Lost

Cinderella's Secret Witch Diaries

(Book 1)

Ron Vitale

Copyright © 2011 Ron Vitale

All rights reserved.

2nd Edition: February 2017

ISBN-13: 978-1542794961

ISBN-10: 154279496X

This book is a work of fiction. Names, characters, places and incidents are the product of the author's imagination or are used fictitiously. Any resemblance to actual events, locales or persons, living or dead, is coincidental.

Visit Ron Vitale's website at www.RonVitale.com

To Becca,

May you make your own magic, find love and re-write the fairy tales to have your own happily ever after.

Also by Ron Vitale

Stolen: Cinderella's Secret Witch Diaries (Book 2)

Found: Cinderella's Secret Witch Diaries (Book 3)

Faith: The Jovian Gate Chronicles (Book 1)

The Jovian Gate Chronicles: Short Story Collection

Awakenings: A Witch's Coven (Book 1)

Betrayals: A Witch's Coven (Book 2)

Dorothea's Song

January 2

Dear Fairy Godmother,

Although I am a fool to believe you will ever read these words, I begin this diary in the hope of reaching you. I need your help. Tonight is the twelfth anniversary of my Mother's passing, and I have decided to write to you because I am distraught and sorrowful. I wish that she were still here to comfort me, but she is not, and my heart still aches for her.

In the dozen years since my mother's death, you are the closest I have come to a Mother, as you once rescued me. I have need of your listening ear tonight, for my life is filled with uncertainty. I send these words out to you as a most fervent prayer. With magic beyond what I may know, I conjure the hope that my imaginary correspondence will take flight and that these words will whisper themselves to you as I share with you a story I have longed to tell.

On the night my Mother died, she carried me into her bed, sick as she was, and held me close. Father was away on business, not to return for weeks. A fever had taken us, and I remember how weak I felt. Mother cuddled me in her arms and put a damp cloth on my forehead to cool me. I was soothed and settled back against her, listening to the crackling of the fire.

"Would you like to hear a story about the Silver Fox?" Her voice calmed me.

"Who is that, Mamma?" I asked.

"He is the Faerie Lord who visits our world from time to time to bestow magic on the land."

I nodded and fought hard not to drift into sleep, unaware that this would be the last time my Mother and I would be together. At eight years of age, I thought the world still such a beautiful place. She took the cloth from my forehead and began her tale. Over the years, I have forgotten some parts, but tonight I will retell the story to you in the hope of keeping my Mother's memory alive. If I stop writing and listen, I can almost hear her voice as she told me her tale...

***

"Once in a great while, the Faerie Lord came to the world of men and played in the grass and fields, looking for amusement and companionship."

I looked up at my mother's face and asked, "What did he look like?"

"He resembled a fox. Yet his fur was not rust-colored but silver and bright." She ran her fingers through my hair and glanced longingly out the window. "He chanced upon the house of a young woman who was unhappy in her marriage, for her husband was often away. On seeing her so sad as she dug in her garden, the Faerie Lord shifted into the body of a man and trundled down a hill, unused to balancing on two human legs. He rolled to an embarrassing stop and quite surprised the young woman."

"How did the Faerie Lord change from a fox to a man, and was he hurt?" I woke up a bit and wanted to know.

"Men and faeries can be foxes inside, but his magic was strong and true, so he was unhurt." She paused, and seeing me content with her answer, continued. "He rubbed a bump on his head and smiled at the young woman.

"Standing up and a little surprised, she brushed the dirt off her hands and asked, 'Dear Sir, are you well?'

"He smiled at her with a small devilish grin and winked. 'I am now, for I have met you.' He bowed and from out behind his back he handed her a bunch of wild flowers."

'I cannot accept these,' she backed away and headed toward the house, 'I am married.'

"He put the flowers behind his back, and they vanished from sight. He then bowed, but before taking his leave he knelt and kissed the spot in the dirt where the young woman had been digging. She watched him go, and that night, in the hour before dawn, a beautiful pink rose bush grew and blossomed.

"The next day he returned and again offered her his smile and flowers. She again told him to go away, and he did, but again kissed the ground and whispered into the soil with a smile. The second night another beautiful rose bush grew next to the pink roses of the previous evening. On the third day, she expected his return, but he did not show himself. She wondered what had happened to him and secretly missed him, hoping he would come see her again.

"That night, after midnight, she awoke in bed, hearing an animal scratching at the front door. She gathered her garments and dressed, looking outside. There in the garden was a large silver fox seemingly waiting for her. She walked with caution toward it…"

"Did it bite her?" I interrupted.

7

"The fox did something she did not expect. He changed into a man. As a man, he walked up to her and then looked up at the sky, searching until he found what he wanted. Taking his hands, he cupped them and raised his arms so the moon appeared to be resting in his palms."

'The roses were not enough,' he said. 'But here is the moon that I give to you.'

"Quiet and tentative in her response, a slow smile broke across her face in the moonlight.

"He offered his hands to her and said, 'I have followed you for years and have seen how unhappy you are. Come away with me to the Land of the Fey where you are not married, and I will love you as you deserve for all of your days.'"

"She paused a moment, thinking of her sleeping daughter inside and her husband who was away and the loneliness she had suffered for months upon months and then took his hands in hers, feeling his warmth and smoothness."

* * *

I fell asleep then and never heard the ending to the story. In the morning, my mother was dead. The physician said she had passed in her sleep from the fever that we both had fought against the whole week. I do not remember any of the events following my mother's death, as I was with the sickness for days afterward, which father told me nearly took my life. At such a young age, to lose my mother, the difficulties of that time I still carry with me. But I am not here to write solely on my past woes. I have fresh troubles to resolve. Though, if I be honest, a part of me still wishes my mother were here. I miss her. But that is not to be, as I cannot speak to the dead.

Fairy Godmother, I wish I could have told my Mother's story to you in person because I wonder if you have heard of the Silver Fox, or if he is just the creation of my Mother's fertile imagination. You once cared for me and helped me with your magic. It has been nearly four years since you whisked me to the ball, and I met the Prince, and my supposed happily ever after took place. Why have I not heard from you?

Since that time, much has happened between the Prince and me. In the beginning, his affections were constant and true, but over time, as my usefulness to him declined, so did his attention toward me. His mother, the Queen, has waited for me to produce an heir, and I have failed at so simple a task. The Prince's patience with me is gone, and I ponder on what I may have done wrong, only to realize that what he and I once shared is not as solid as I once thought.

I sit here in my many rooms, alone, in the dark of the night by candlelight, using a pen to alleviate my frustration and woes. Will you hear me, my Fairy

Godmother? I will go to sleep now because I am weary, and I will hope to dream of better days to come in the warm sun.

January 23

Dear Fairy Godmother,

Quite some time has passed since I have been able to write. Several weeks ago my good friend Clarissa came looking for me in a panic. She called and called for me in distress, running into my room with her skirts bundled up in her hands in such a state. There had been an accident, the Prince had been hurt, and one of his men had almost been killed. She rushed the story, and I tried to take it all in. A horse had become spooked, and there had been drinking on the hunt. Horses collided, and one of them reared up into the air and fell on top of a young attendant. In the confusion, the Prince was hit in the shoulder with a wild horse's hooves, but he stood his ground and protected the boy from being further trampled. There was much talk of the Prince's heroic act, but he would hear none of it, saying he was simply happy to have saved the boy.

Several weeks have passed since the accident, and the doctor has informed us that the Prince will recover, but the accident was frightful to us all. The Queen hovered over his bedside like an angel, and I tried to tend to him, like a good wife, but the situation tested my patience, for his mother's disapproval of me was hard to ignore. At times, I have not liked her. She has been controlling and intrusive, insinuating that my inability to bear a child is my fault and due to my social standing and poor background. She has not said this outright, so perhaps I exaggerate, but I feel that she dislikes me and believes that I am not good enough for her son.

The first night after the accident frightened us all, for the Prince was weak and in pain from his broken shoulder and ribs. The Queen knelt by his bed in silence for most of the night.

I sat to the right of the bed, and when the Queen thought me asleep I saw her take her son's hands in hers and whisper, "Please save him, Lord. Please, heal my son."

She rocked back and forth, repeating the chant over and over again, stopping every few moments to wipe the Prince's brow. I pretended to be asleep, embarrassed by the Queen's intense prayers. I had never seen her act with such love before. With my own eyes closed, I reached out to you, Fairy Godmother, and prayed that you would help save the Prince with your fairy magic. I do not know if either of our prayers helped him, but in the early morning hours I could see how tired the Queen was and called for an attendant to assist her.

After the sun rose, a change came over the Prince, and he rested more peacefully. I went back to my chamber to sleep and prepare for the long days ahead. I do not know how long the Queen stayed with the Prince, but when I returned later that morning she was still there. The Prince had opened his eyes and tried to smile, but it was apparent that he had withstood a difficult night.

He thanked both of us for staying with him and excused us, asking that we worry not for him, as he saw how tired we both were. The Queen gently kissed him on the forehead and smiled, leaving him in peace. I withdrew as well, but before I could leave he reached for my hand and squeezed it.

"Thank you for your concern." He held my hand for a moment but let it go quickly. "I suspect many guests will come to visit me. You better get some rest."

I kissed his hand and smiled. "I am happy that you are better."

"My own lack of caution caused the accident, with the rest of the group filled with drink," he said with frustration. "Lucky we were that the boy was not trampled and killed." He pounded a pillow with his good hand. "What an ass I was, boasting of my great hunting skills, and I did not see Charles come behind me."

I remained silent, unsure of how to respond.

"Go rest, as you deserve some peace." He pushed away my hand.

He closed his eyes, distraught with his thoughts, and I left him. I did desire some rest myself. The weeks after the accident were filled, as the Prince foresaw, with visitors coming to wish him well, and I needed to entertain them. I became drained from my duties. Visitors have now left the court after their extended stay to bring cheer and comfort to the Prince. He is no longer confined to his bed, but he walks with slowness and a tenderness that show his injuries are still of concern to him.

His kindness to me over the last few weeks has been constant, and I hope that he does not distance himself from me again. I have spoken at length with Clarissa, and her friendship has helped me during this dark time. But I fear that once the Prince is well enough, I will again be forgotten, like an old shoe. Let me end here before I turn too somber. It is late, and I should sleep.

January 25

Dear Fairy Godmother,

Earlier today Clarissa came to visit me as I practiced my writing. She took my hand and said, "Come with me."

Attempting to argue with or ask for a reason from Clarissa only frustrates her, so I put down my book and followed. She brought me to the kitchens, where I knew that she had matters of importance to speak, as the rest of the royal family never visits this side of the castle.

"I have seen him make advances toward another." Clarissa held my hands firmly in hers. "I do not trust him, and have seen this with my own eyes."

My heart ached at the words. I did not wish to hear any more of what she had seen. "I fear to ask you to tell me more."

"He plans to be unfaithful to you. I have seen it." Clarissa saw me turn away.

"I do not wish to hear any more. I truly wish you to cease this talk as it pains me to hear the words." I pulled away from her and started back to my room.

"You are a Princess and do not deserve such treatment." Clarissa noticed several of the kitchen hands turn toward us, so she lowered her voice. "Do not allow him to treat you so!"

She followed after me and grabbed at my arm. I stopped, covered my hands, and took a breath. "I came from ashes and dirt not born of royal blood. Nothing I say will convince him to do other than he desires."

"If you remain silent, then you are complicit and he will take you as weak of will, which I know that you are not." She placed her hands together in prayer. "Please, confront him before he has his way with this woman."

"The time for action has already passed." I lowered my head and began to cry. "Do you not understand? I am weak and unable to stand against him for fear that I will be abandoned."

Clarissa remained quiet and she came closer and spoke low. "You have proof of this?"

"Proof enough as my own two eyes have seen a sight I wish they had not." I tried to stop crying as I did not enjoy showing my vulnerability and fear, but could not.

"What do you plan to do?" she asked.

"I do not know. I truly do not know."

Cinderella's Secret Diary (Book 1: Lost)

Such is the news within my heart that I share with you. I cannot go back to my father as my stepmother and her daughters still rule him. If I leave here, I have no subsistence of my own to survive and know of no relatives to take me in and shelter me. I have twenty years, am married and trapped in a prison of my own making. When you helped me attend the ball and I met the Prince, I imagined my life changed forever and that goodness and light would reign over the rest of my days. Yet the darkness that has descended over me is complete, and I am afraid.

I have considered leaving here, dream of it each night, but where would I go? I beg of you in my hour of need to please hear me. I am in despair. Aid me with your magic and whisk me away so that I can have time to think and place my thoughts, rather than be afraid of my own husband! His mood is not to be swayed when he is choleric, and I fear to stand against him. He has made his wishes clear to me these last years. My Mother, if she were here, what would she say to me? I often wonder.

She could counsel me if she were still here, but she is not, and my only true and deserved friend is the lovely Clarissa. Unmarried and beholden to her father, she has not the power to save me. Thus my thoughts of fancy turn to you in the hope that you will come to me. I beg of you to use your magic and help me in my need.

What foolishness I continue to entertain, I do not know. I truly do not know. If there be faerie magic, let it come to rescue me.

January 26

Cinderella,

Help from magick lies within each heart
if to claim it as your own is what you seek.
Look and search within before you start
as you must free your mind to reach its peak.

Dear Fairy Godmother,

What magic have you used to reach out and write back to me in this very book? My dearest fairy Godmother, you have discovered a way to answer me! I want to sit down and write back to you, but your words are so few and elusive. You have asked for me to free my mind, and I will do so in the hope that we will soon be reconciled. When I first saw the letters and words in my book, I feared that someone had secreted into my chamber and wrote the words to play with me, but I see that is not possible, as the words glow soft in a silvery light. No quill and ink could make those marks. The words were created with magic pure and true. I am excited and happy that you can hear me. If you can read what I write here, then I will share with you the stories of my days in the hope that you will continue to communicate with me.

I hear noise outside my door. I am sorry, but I must go.

January 27

Dear Fairy Godmother,

I woke this morning not feeling well. There is a sickness that has afflicted many in the castle. The weather has been cold, but not cold enough for snow, and yet I have a chill that I cannot rid myself of. My mind wanders back to this diary, and I often question whether your note to me still exists. I often open the book to the page, rub my hand over the words you wrote, and smile. I do not know how or when we will be together, but you have charged me with a task that I have set myself to.

Yet I am here, and my task is to free my mind, so I will attempt to do so in these days of winter and darkness. Here at the castle, life is quiet as the sickness has caused many to fall ill. I suspect that I have the illness because my head is light, and I find that I am often tired. I try hard to free my mind and imagine what it would be like to have the freedom to not worry about my husband or the Queen as I go about my daily routine. I imagine that I would have peace and that new ideas would come to me, for when I am alone, I am wont to dream of travel and seeing new cultures. If I were to open the dams within my mind, a rush of thought would come to me of which I am still much afraid. I do wish to travel and see France with its operas, plays and art.

I know not how to achieve these dreams when there are such obstacles in my path. I truly do not. Last night after all had gone to sleep, I brought out the glass slippers that you gave me, and I put them on. With eyes closed, I imagined that you stood beside me, and we talked about other girls you had helped. You would think me silly in my nightclothes standing in front of the mirror wearing the glass slippers that I treasure as my own. I would write more, but to bed I must go as I feel tired and weak.

I pray that I will dream of your return to me and that when I awake all will be made clear!

February 10

Dear Fairy Godmother,

I have been very sick. Truth be told, I did not think I was going to live. A strong fever and cough weakened and sickened me, as well as many in the castle. I lay in bed, day after day, with a high fever, unable to get up, and feeling so tired and delirious. I wanted to write to you but could not as I was too weak. Perhaps a week ago Clarissa came to wake me, for I did not get up in the morning. I could tell from the worried look on her face that she was upset. I felt trapped in my own body, but could not gather the strength to rise out of bed.

She felt my forehead and then covered me. Yet the cold would not leave my bones no matter how many covers she placed me under. Clarissa, my dear, dear friend, called the King's doctor, who came to examine me. He let out some of my blood to remove the sickness, and told me to stay in bed and rest.

For seven long days, I stayed in bed, sick, and feverish. Time passed oddly as I lost track of the days and drifted in and out of sleep. One day I had a surge of energy that focused my faculties so much so that a sense of clarity came over me. Fearing that I would die, I devised a plan to give Clarissa my diaries in order that the Prince never read them. In a fit of stubbornness, I tried to rise out of bed and tell Clarissa that I had to give her my diaries and that I needed her help to keep them secret from the Prince and his Mother.

Poor Clarissa! I can only imagine what she thought of me in my deranged state. I have not had a chance to talk to her since that time, as she has been busy taking care of others who are sick. Two of the more elderly servants have died from this dreaded sickness, and many others have fallen ill. I have only been up and about for a day now, and I still find it difficult to walk. I must take my time and am trying to build up my strength.

The Prince came to see me several times, and he did stay with me for a long while. He was kind and sweet. The one day he sat by my bed for hours, not saying anything as I moaned in my feverish state, but it was encouraging to see him sitting there. He had several large maps on his lap and it looked like he was studying them.

Later that day I heard him ask for more logs to be put on the fire and he asked for hot tea to be brought to me. I tried to drink it, but could not lift the cup to my lips. He sat next to me, held the cup, and I drank a few sips at a time.

"Thank you for your help." I lay back on my pillow and rested. The room appeared larger to me, and I had a difficult time concentrating, as every item swayed to a strange motion that I could not control.

"You took care of me when I had injured myself and did not complain or admonish me for my antics." He sat back in his chair, putting the cup of tea on a tray.

"Do you remember how happy we were when we first met?" I believe the fever caused me to speak more openly.

"I recall how magical you were with your dress, the glass slippers and your charming smile." He rubbed the beard on his chin.

"Are you not happy with me?" I turned to face him directly. "Have I disappointed you in some way?"

He turned from me and picked up his cup of tea, lingering on the sip as he gathered his thoughts. "Must we speak of this now?"

"I would like to know…"

He interrupted me before I could finish and said, "The doctor informed me that you are in a delicate state and that your rest is paramount."

"Of course." I remained silent and closed my eyes, trying to hold back my tears.

He did not say anything else, and after a few minutes of my silent crying, he stood up and left the room without a word. A part of me had warmed to him, for his actions were kind and thoughtful, but a thoughts of deeper motive rose to the surface of my mind, and I wondered if guilt caused him to care for me.

Now, days later, I have had much time to think while recuperating, and I have come to a decision. I had thought about withholding my opinion, even from myself, as possibly the effects of the fever still hold sway over me, but I know that is not the case. Freely I will say that I dislike the Prince at times and think he can be an insensitive man.

He and I met when I was 16 years of age and my knowledge of the world was remote and naïve. Yet at 20, am I truly much more informed? I think not. Rather I realize a truth that I had not wanted to speak before: I wanted to escape my life under my stepmother. The Prince needed a woman at his side for appearances and to have his children. I have performed my role extremely well as a Princess, learning all that was necessary to fulfill my duties. I have been dignified and graceful, supporting the King and Queen, showing that I am worthy of my status. Now I question what my future in this family will be. I wonder if I will be forever trapped in my fear.

My hand tires from writing so much. Perhaps I should go and have some dinner. Wherever you are, Fairy Godmother, I wish you well.

February 11

Clarissa came to visit me this morning, and our talk turned toward my future. We wandered off to a quiet part of the castle and sat by a fire talking. Clarissa looked at the condition of my dress and shook her head. "Your clothes are in such disrepair. What would you do without a friend like me?"

I smiled, and for the first time in days felt more myself with my returned strength. Staring at the fire for a few moments, I asked, "Would it not be wonderful if we could travel the world together?"

"Of course it would. What is your plan?" Clarissa sat down in her chair and leaned toward the fire.

"I have no plan. I am just dreaming. The Prince continues to ignore me, although I have tried to talk with him, but I suspect he simply wishes to live his life as he may and keep me as his public wife. I am not happy with my life and would enjoy traveling to experience art, music and..."

"Love!" Clarissa interrupted me and laughed. "You would not be the first wife to have her own understandings with a gentleman."

"I would rather not. I weary of the challenges of love."

Clarissa kept quiet and then replied, "I wish I had such a problem."

"You will find your gentleman soon enough."

Clarissa stood up and walked over to the fire. "I worry about you. You are still so young and yet your joy is so slight of late."

"I hardly see the Prince any longer, and the times we do spend together are more for his duty to produce an heir." I fiddled with a bow on my dress. "My standing with him is clear and, I cannot change his mind."

Our conversation shifted to talk of the upcoming ball, and yet as I write this the question keeps coming back to me. How could I travel, and where would I go? I cannot simply walk out the castle gates. My knowledge of politics and the world of men is limited, yet even I have heard the rumors of conflict in Europe. I have tried to solve this riddle but cannot. When I look upon the playing field, I see that the main power is the Queen. She has left me enough alone these long days as I recover from my sickness, but I suspect that she will call me for a visit soon.

What would you have me do, Fairy Godmother? Weeks have passed since I have last heard from you. What should I do?

February 12

It is early, and the snow still falls outside as I write this, but I am wrapped up nicely in some warm covers, glancing from time to time at the world of white. The snow began yesterday afternoon, and I watched as it fell, heavy and near silent. Though later the wind did pick up and snow blew all around. After dinner yesterday, Clarissa and I snuck outside to walk around the palace gardens. The trees and the trimmed bushes were blanketed in the soft fluffy whiteness. We did not go very far, as we were both cold, but I did make time to talk with Clarissa and properly thank her being such a good friend.

She and I walked arm in arm through the snow, and we were both amazed at how beautiful everything looked. A fresh blanket of white covered the palace grounds, making the world quiet and new. We walked in silence and returned to the castle to have some tea with bread and butter. We were alone, warm and safe. I looked at my best friend and asked, "Are you happy?"

She laughed and sipped her tea. "I suspect that your question is more than 'Am I happy with my tea and biscuit?'"

"You know me well." I leaned back and took a sip of the warm tea. It brought courage to my weary body. "If you were not my lady-in-waiting, what would you want to do with your life?"

She thought for a moment, scratching her nose. "I would travel to lands beyond this castle and its familiar walls." She brushed crumbs off of her dress and pointed outside. "I have never been too far but I have heard such amazing stories. Instead, I sit here like a farm animal, waiting for my father to sell me off to the highest bidder."

A pained look crossed her face. "I am older now and my father worries that I will not make a good match as I am strong willed and difficult. He tolerates my behavior but for how much longer? I fear…" She let her words trail off and she looked away.

I waited to see if she would continue but she did not. "You are still young and I daresay that you are more beautiful than me. A man who finds you will be lucky to have such a pretty and independent-thinking wife."

"Thank you for your kind words." She smiled and drank more tea.

I gathered my courage and chanced to speak the truth. "I want to tell you that I am not happy here." I forced myself to continue. "I have made a decision to travel, but I am still not certain if I am courageous enough to find a way to make my wish come true."

I did not know what else to say, but then had an idea came to me. We both felt trapped in our situations, but that would not last forever. My idea rolled off my tongue and said, "I want you to come to France with me."

Clarissa's face lit up with wondrous excitement and she asked so many questions that I could not keep up with her.

If I could convince the Prince to go to France in the Spring, then I would need my lady-in-waiting to help me. Such a trip would be difficult but not impossible, as we were not that far from the Channel. We could ride by carriage, hire a boat, and then head to France. Yet once there, I did not know how long it would take by carriage to get to the capital. I suspected that all could be arranged. I would have to figure the details out. A carriage to Dover would take a day, but I had heard the stories of the rough Channel waters and how sometimes travelers would have to wait several days for calm waters. But would Calais to Paris consist of another day's travel by carriage? I did not know the geography exactly, but I knew I need not solve all the details at once. What mattered is that I had an idea.

Clarissa and I talked for a good while about our plans for the Spring, and it was very enjoyable. I was happy to see her smile again and for her to have some hope that all was not lost. The two of us would work together and make my plan come to life. How to get the Prince to agree might be difficult. We would have to see.

I must end my writing here. I am not ashamed to write this but I need my rest and am lying down to sleep some more. Bonne nuit! (See, already I am practicing my French.)

Dear Cinderella,

You have begun to free your mind and see the possibilities that can be if you allow them to grow and bear fruit. If you wonder how to convince your Prince to go to Paris, ask yourself this: Who must he listen to and what does She want above all else?

I am proud of you and see you have made much progress. Soon we will be together.

Yours,

Fairy Godmother

February 15

You wrote to me again! I am so pleased, for each day I wake hoping to see another magical note from you in my diary. I want to see you and wonder how that can come to be as I do not know where you are. Are you far away from this land, and do you use your magic to see me here? I long to know more, for I miss you and hope that you are well. When you write me next, I implore you to tell me how we can be in each other's company once again.

I have much to share with you. My mind wanders to the divergence ahead for the Prince and me. I see us as walking separate paths, and I do not know if I am prepared to accept the burden of that choice. With reflection, I am frightened and still beholden to my duty for what I should do. I will need Clarissa's guidance and friendship to help me through the difficult times ahead.

As I write this, it is in the middle of the night. I am alone, and the quiet is soothing to me. While in this solitude, I am able to write in peace without any distractions from others or even my own doubts.

On the table to my left are my glass slippers. I prize those shoes above all else as they are a reminder to me that you did come to help me and that your magic is solid and true. When you came to assist me, you asked that I gather a pumpkin, mice and lizards. I followed your instructions, and with your magic you turned the pumpkin into my carriage, the mice into horses, and the lizards into footmen. You then waved your hands around me and turned my dirty clothes into a beautiful gown with the most wondrous jewels. But then you gave me the glass slippers etched with small wildflowers. Their beauty bewildered me, and they remain after all these years. Before I went to the castle that momentous night, you had me promise that I would return by midnight, and as I rushed away from the ball everything turned back to what it was before, but not the slippers. They remained.

The famous story of how the Prince found one of my glass slippers and had all the ladies try it on is now so engrained in the folklore of the town that even little children know of it. Yet many do not recall that I had the second glass slipper. I kept it as a reminder of you and on the day that the Prince came to my father's home he asked that we all try the glass slipper on. When I did, it fit perfectly, and I pulled its mate out of my pocket and showed it to him. The amazement on his face is hard to forget. I could not tell then if he were upset or just surprised, but now I know that he had thought I was special and would marry me to show his friends and Mother what a great match he had found on his own.

Initially, I think he was taken aback at my rags, but the magic surrounding the story won him over. He heard the rumors of the fairy and the powerful spells that changed my clothes, and he warmed to that mystique. I think he wanted your magic to also grace his life, choosing me not so much for love but for my connection to such wonderment. I do not mind all of that now. Too much time has passed, and yet the glass slippers still remain. Why they have not turned into dust or disappeared I do not know, and do not question. I have not the chance to thank you in person for the gift, yet I shall write my thanks here now. Thank you, my dear Fairy Godmother, for a gift that has helped me through my struggles. They fit just as well now as they did then, and, on occasion, I wear them to special balls and amaze the attendees, for they also expected the glass slippers to disappear or to wear or break.

I have examined the shoes closely over the years, running my fingers over the etched flowers and the small fox that looks to be frolicking in the flowers. Often when I am in distress, I gather them in my arms and trace the flowers with my fingers, feeling the grooves with my fingers, and, maybe it is my imagination, but I feel warmth and energy in the shoes. They always cheer me up when I am sad or lonely and afraid. Holding the shoes and feeling the touch of them on my skin brings me a sense of completeness that warms my heart. Over the years I have tried to lend them to people, but they simply do not fit. Even my dearest Clarissa cannot wear them, and we share shoes and clothing all through the year. She is unable to wear them, as they simply do not fit.

I do not know what magic you put into these slippers, but I thank you. Fairy and goodness and godmother to me, I wish I knew more about you. I wish I could learn more about who you really are. I have talked to my friends, stepmother and stepsisters, but they know nothing of you.

I sit here in the warmth of a fire in the middle of winter, and I look at the glass slippers. I can see the fire reflecting in them and I can touch them. They are real. They are a symbol of what you once gave to me. They remain. Solid and true and lasting.

To sleep now, I must go as it will be light soon. I need to ponder your question and put into action my plan, for Paris awaits. Thank you for all you have done for me. I pray you are well and we will be reconciled soon. Good night!

February 21

Dear Fairy Godmother,

The Queen now knows that I wish to speak with her, and I hope to have an audience with her soon. Although I am her son's wife, my status does not allow for me to speak with her at a time of my choosing. Rather, I have placed the proper request, and patient I must now be. When I shall be called to speak with her, I do not know. I hope and pray it will be soon.

Clarissa is here for me. I am telling her that I am coming. I need to go. I will be back. I promise.

Late in the day on February 21

The sun has risen, and we have only just returned from the midwinter ball. Clarissa had asked that I attend with her because she wanted to help enliven my spirits. It is true that I have been especially low of late. She knew, too, that the Prince would perform one or two obligatory dances and then sit at a table in a far corner and talk with his friends, drinking until the ball ended

Tonight, I danced to forget my woes, hoping that the music would transport me to another state of mind. I have seen with my own eyes how easy losing one's self to the music, food and drink can be, as many forget to return. I could do the same easily and forget all my dreams and just live for those moments. I have seen many other young women of court lose their way, become lost with their men on the side, their drinking, or their lust for jewels and wealth. I believe that my heart is true and that I have not yet lost my way, for I remember what I still want out of life.

There is an ache in my heart and I know that my destiny is open and filled with purpose, but as to what that purpose is, I have not yet discovered. I hear a calling to travel to France. I feel compelled to go there. If I want to go to France with Clarissa, I need to convince the Queen or my entire plan will fall apart. I await the Queen to call upon me, and I shall see if my hope will come to fruition.

Now I must to bed as I need to rest. Good night.

February 27

The Queen has yet to answer my request to speak with her, but I have been forced to talk with the Prince about my desire to visit France. After dinner, he came to me and we shared enough pleasantries to be friendly. He walked with me and said, "You have recovered well from the sickness."

I nodded and replied, "I have been well for weeks now. Thank you."

He appeared agitated as he paced back and forth in my room. "I must be frank with you."

His sudden forthrightness surprised me. "Of course, my Lord."

"I hear rumor that you wish to travel to France in the Spring." He stopped pacing and faced me. "Is this true?"

I wondered how he had learned of my desire, but Clarissa and I have openly spoken of the topic, so rumors would have spread. "Yes, I would."

He remained silent for a time and then said, "I would enjoy taking you to Paris. I truly would." I thought his emotion honest and open. However, he continued. "But I cannot."

He face turned red and blotches appeared on his neck. I did not correctly read why he was upset. I simply blundered onward and asked, "Why are you unable to take a party to Paris? You are the Prince."

I could see him bite his tongue, but I still did not know what had bothered him so much.

He turned away from me and walked toward a window to stare out at the darkness.

Instead of remaining quiet, I pushed onward. "I do not understand. Why are you not able to go?"

"Why?" He spun around, and I could see a sudden red rage in his face. "I, too, have wanted to go to France this summer, but my father commanded me not to go."

In puzzlement, I stood confused. I did not understand.

"Will you not share your mind with me?" I asked.

"The King is afraid for his precious throne. Rumors from the mainland reached us months ago. Napoleon Bonaparte rises to power in France. It is said that he dreams of ruling the world, and he is no friend to England."

I felt ignorant and reduced as an insignificant insect lost in a vast world. In my grand plans, I had not thought about world governments and politics. I only wanted to go see the beautiful city of Paris and to have fun with Clarissa.

The Prince could see that I had been ignorant of France's internal politics, and he did not let it go. He laughed at me. "You are thinking of your precious balls and the great time you would have in Paris while I went hunting and stayed out of your way. Do you think I cannot see through you? We are married long enough for me to know your schemes."

Anger welled up inside of me, and I could not silence myself. "Do not talk that way to me. I am your wife and Princess to the realm."

He laughed harder. "Princess," the acid in his voice dripped with sarcasm, "I have been very patient. You have produced no heir to me and now you try to order me around?"

He picked up a gaming billiard on a table and threw it against the wall and it ricocheted in the opposite direction. "I am tired of being told what to do."

And he left. I stayed seated for quite some time and did not know what to do. He had never expressed to me such fury before. I had pushed him too far. I do not know where he went, but I was certain that he did not wish for me to come after him. I left him alone and worried how the future would unfold. Could he be rid of me? I had no knowledge of the law and of his duty and responsibility. Could he pick another woman to be his wife so that he could produce an heir if I was barren? What would then become of me?

My fears have piled upon themselves, and I have spun myself into a dreadful fit of insecurity. My plans have dissolved into nothingness before my eyes, and I am worried. I do not even know where to begin. Let me settle myself for a moment. Oh, Fairy Godmother, I feel trapped, and for the first time I am aware of the full magnitude of my problems.

I have not been able to see Clarissa because she is away with her father visiting cousins. She will not be back for another week. I wish Clarissa were here. I want to talk with her. She would help me. She would know what to do. I am so tired, confused, and my mind is full of troublesome thoughts. I am spinning in circles, and I want this all to go away.

March 4

I am more at peace now. I want to write about what I have done before all of my memories fade away. I am here in my room now, and it has been some time since the Prince and I last talked. We have not seen each other since our disagreement. He has left the castle and I do not know where he travels.

At a loss about what to do, I went to Church and I knelt down and prayed to you. I prayed that you would come find me and rescue me. It is the same old prayer and story. I am not ashamed to admit that I cried. I was alone and no one saw me. I prayed and no answer came. I have begged you to come to me, but you do not. You have written to me and given me some advice, but I have not heard from the Queen. She will not see me, and I do not know why.

When I left the small Church, I went out into the forest at night. If you were not to come to me, then I would try to find you. I have heard all the stories of the fairies that live in the woods. Stories parents tell their children to explain why milk curdles and meat spoils. I gathered a small pack and went off in the night to search of you. The guards know my ways by now, and they would have stopped me, but a few years ago Clarissa showed me a secret way out of the castle. It is not the most comfortable of paths, but I can avoid being seen if I use it. The journey through the now-defunct moat is the worst part, but even that is not too demanding. The way is tricky, to be sure, but not impossible.

Once out of the castle, I could see a waning moon, one or two days past full, hanging high in the sky. It was not too cold, just a touch of chill in the air. The light from the moon was enough to guide my way so that I could find the path to the forest. There is a trail that leads through the woods, and I have been through the forest before, during the daylight. But the rumors and stories say that in the dark, after midnight, the fey come out to do their mischief or to help those in need.

I stood at the edge of the woods and I stopped, for I was afraid. I admit it. I turned around and could hear no one behind me. I did not fear that any wild animal would attack me, but I was still afraid. I truly did not know who or what I might encounter in the woods so late at night. Clarissa might have danced into the woods, as she is such an adventurous soul. Me, I was afraid. I did not know if I were more afraid of what I would find or that I would not find anything. It was possible that I could simply go through the forest and come out cold and tired. But there was a moment of possibility in which I imagined what would happen if I were to find you, to see you in your element, and to find a way to connect with you. That insane bit of hope burned inside my mind and warmed me. I could have stood there, at the edge, for a long, long time, relieved in my hopes. I so wanted for everything to become revealed to me so that I could understand where I needed to go and what I should do in life.

In the dim moonlight, I could see some buds of flowers coming up out of the dirt by the side of the trail, and the path ahead looked clear and somewhat used. I took a step forward and then, after some time, another.

I clenched my hands at my side and walked ahead, hoping that I would find my salvation inside the forest. I felt colder in going into the woods, but maybe that was just my fear. Although my path was covered by trees, the light of the moon allowed me to see, and a light wind was all I could hear. All around me were trees and undergrowth, but I did not sense any danger. I was more frightened than I think I had ever been before. I was surrounded by darkness, and there were no animals or creatures stirring in the night, but I sensed that something was watching me. Maybe it was just my fear speaking to me, and I kept shivering, so I walked onward, not knowing what to expect.

I had never been far from home. In truth, I had never left the town in which I was born. We moved after my mother died but it was only from one part of our town to another. After the Prince married me, I moved into the castle, yet I still have not been out of town. The trail that I took led North, onward to the capital. How many people had ridden in carriages on the path that I now walked? More than I would ever know. It was not unusual for people to come to our town, but when my friends and I were growing up, the woods were enchanted with faeries, and the trees spoke the language of magic. I walked onward with purpose and increased my pace, afraid to stop, for I was certain that some creature out of my darkest imagination would grab at my ankles and pull me deep into the earth.

I do not know how long and far I walked, but after some time I realized the folly of my plan. I had no food, water, clothes, or a lantern. Alone and in the woods, any band of thieves or gypsies could find me and I would be regretting my decision to explore the woods in the dark of night in the tail end of winter. I must admit now, in looking back, that I made a poor choice. I could have easily fallen and hurt myself in the dark and, alone, I would not have been heard calling for help. Or, if I were heard, I doubt it would be someone wanting to help me.

The trail before me continued, and behind there was only darkness. My trail had no end in sight, and I was leaving all I knew to chase after a dream of finding you. I was alone. Suddenly, I caught a movement out of the corner of my eye, and turned. A fox, looking silver in the moonlight, ran across the trail.

It stopped for a moment to peer at me, its tongue hanging out as it panted, and then it rushed on its way.

The night had turned colder and I stopped. I could hear water nearby. Running water such as what would come from a small creek. To my left, I could see a small branch of the trail that headed off toward the sound of the running water. I had only a small amount of courage left within. If I did not go to look at the water, I would regret my midnight excursion, and all would be in vain. Yet if I went forward, I thought I would make a good compromise between my fear and the foolish bravery I exhibited. I had walked a while and found nothing. If I looked out at the water and saw no faeries or water sprites, then I could turn around and head back to the comfort of the castle.

I followed the path and the sound of running water became louder. Up ahead, the trees cleared, and I saw a small creek that was maybe four horses in width across. The water flowed quickly, and off in the distance was the gentle sound of a small falls. The moonlight shone across the water, which splashed over the rocks. Nothing else moved. I saw no other animals or sign of any people and, for a moment, I crouched down and just stared out at the water. I was happy. Yes, I was cold, but I was enjoying the solitude and, I do not know why, but I had an idea. I walked down the small embankment, careful not to slip and fall on the rocks, and I knelt by the edge of the creek. I took the pack off my back and opened it up. Inside my glass slippers reflected the beauty of the moonlight. I held them in my right hand and carefully dipped my fingers into the cold creek. I waited and nothing happened. Then, to be certain, I stood up and took off my boots and put on the glass slippers. I stood up and put my arms out and up at the moon and…. Nothing happened.

I closed my eyes and focused. I felt foolish. I opened my eyes, and to my right I saw the fox again. He looked at me, so close now, watching me with a curious look on his face. He stared a moment, made a noise that sounded a bit like laughter and then rushed off into the night. I suspect if there were someone watching me then he would have done the same and laughed with much merriment, as I must have appeared to be a fool. A princess, alone in the night, standing on the edge of a creek with glass slippers on, praying up at the moon to her Fairy Godmother.

I put my arms down, changed back into my boots, and took one last long look at the creek at night. I closed my eyes, and I called out to you, and then I did something I am a bit ashamed to write about, but it is late and I need to write it. I called out to you with all my voice, asking for help. I do not know what words I used, but I called out, praying that you would hear and answer me. Or that one of the elite faerie guards would fly down and land on my nose, wondering why I put such a loud noise to voice.

I closed my eyes and cried, and then pounded the side of my fist into a tree. It felt good to release my anger. After a while, I stopped, put my slippers away, and then headed back to the castle. I heard no one on the way back. No fox disturbed me. All was quiet, and I snuck back through the moat and the secret door, and came to my bed chamber. It is very late, and in another hour the kitchen staff will begin lighting the fire for the day, and preparation for the morning meal will begin.

I have already decided that I will feign fatigue, sleep late, and forget about my problems and the world. Tonight I truly thought that the faeries or you, my Fairy Godmother, would come to me and I would be swept away in a river of light and magic. Music would fill the air, and lights from all the colors of the rainbow would shine around me like a mid-day summer sun during an outdoor festival, but none of that happened. Worse, I think I made a fool of myself, and am alone. I will think on whether I will tell Clarissa of my stupidity and what I have done.

What I truly do not understand is that I have, at times, felt the magic within the glass slippers. Why did they not speak for me? I put all my thoughts and energy into calling out to you, but there was nothing. No reply. The hope that lives within me is telling me that in the winter the faeries do not live in the woods but that they will be back in the summer time. And the more I think on this, the more I am ashamed at what I am asking, for there is no sense in it.

You have written to me, but when I need you the most you have not answered. Does something prevent you from reaching me? I have done as you have asked and have freed my mind. I have spoken with the Prince, but he denies me, and I have tried to see the Queen, but she will not allow it. Please, help me.

March 24

Much has happened, and I am not sure where I should start the story. If you had a hand in making my dream come true, I thank you so. I will be packing for Paris later today and will be on the road by tomorrow. I am amazed at how fast events have transpired.

Several days after I last wrote, the Queen summoned me to her chamber after dinner. My long wait to speak with her had reached its conclusion. Surprisingly, she invited me to her private chamber. When I entered, she waved her attendants away and walked around the room, comparing different swaths of cloth to a dress by a table. She was without her wig and makeup, and I had never seen such an intimate side of the Queen before. I must admit that I would not have recognized her. She muttered to herself and glanced over at me and then said, "Which pattern do you like best?"

I approached her and curtsied low, looking at the pieces of material in her hand. "I like the blue one." She handed me the cloth. I held it in my hands and was impressed with the pattern's simplicity and smoothness.

"I like that color, too." She went about her business, putting away the pattern samples and then sat in her chair. "My son is off again, I hear."

I remained quiet for a few moments, unsure of how to answer and then replied, "Your Majesty, I believe it is my fault."

She laughed. "My son is often upset these days, and I doubt you are solely to blame." She poured her own cup of tea and motioned for me to have some. I accepted, oddly unsure why the Queen served me.

"If my sources are true, I hear that your argument with my son centers around your desire to visit Paris this Spring. Is that correct?"

I was hesitant to reply.

She put her tea cup down and looked me up and down. "Do you mind if I am frank with you?" She did not wait for me to respond. "You are important to me because you can bear the heir to the throne. If you work with me, then I will support you. Understood?"

I nodded, at a loss for words.

"Now tell me, am I correct that you and my son argued about your desire to visit Paris?"

"Yes, Your Majesty." I had not touched my cup of tea yet as my hands were too unsteady.

"It is as I expected then." The Queen took a look sip of tea and stared out the window, thinking. "I love my son. I truly do, but he would do better for us all if he were not so difficult. Would you not agree?"

I blushed and kept my eyes down as I suspected a verbal trap.

The Queen smiled. "You are a wise woman to keep your feelings close about a mother's son. I respect you for that."

"Your Majesty?" The words escaped me before I could contain them.

"Finally, you speak up." She cocked her eye at me and waited.

"If there is war between England and France, how can we go to Paris?"

"Before I answer that, will you make me a promise?"

I did not need to think long. I needed the Queen's help. "Yes, Your Majesty, I will listen to you and make a promise."

"Good." She walked over to me and put her hand on my shoulder. She had never touched me before, and I flinched in fear. She ignored my reaction and asked, "Will you go see a woman who lives in Paris? She will help you with your problem."

"How can she help me?"

"Over the years I have sent other ladies to her and then they have been able to have children. She is known throughout Europe in the right circles. I only wish she lived in England."

Fear remained foremost on my mind, and I was afraid to admit it to the Queen. "Will it hurt?"

"No, you will only need to drink some potions several times a week."

"Then, yes, I will promise to do what the woman says so that I can become pregnant." I felt more at ease, as I had feared surgery or some heathen ritual.

Seeing my discomfort ease, the Queen sat back down in her chair. "You are valuable to me because you are married to my son." She stopped and then took me in with her gaze. "But if you ever are disloyal to him, I will not be forgiving."

I made to stand up and leave and she put out her hand, motioning for me to stay seated. She had not finished with me. "When my son comes back to the fold, and he will soon, I will need for you to make peace with him, for having a child requires the two of you to be on speaking terms."

"Your Majesty, I understand." I kept my hands folded in my lap for fear she would see how frightened I was of her.

"Now you may retire for the evening."

I stood, curtsied low, and left the room, backing toward the door as I had been taught to do. When I left, I hurried back to my room and have been writing since. I am filled with immense joy that my dream will be a reality, and it seems that I did not have to work hard to convince the Queen because she had plans for me already. I am concerned, yet that is for me to worry about

Cinderella's Secret Diary (Book 1: Lost)

another day. I will read for a while before bed and then try to dream of the wonders of Paris. Bonne nuit!

March 26

Dear Cinderella,

My distance from you is the reason for my infrequent letters. You are my dearest and I love you more than you will ever know. The challenges are great to cast out my thoughts to you and have them appear here. I am off helping other women and will come back to you soon. You must have faith in me and trust when I tell you that I have never forgotten you.

I have not much strength left, but I must warn you before I go. The Queen's plan to send you to a woman she has heard about in France concerns me. You must avoid seeing her, for she is a witch of great power. Tread with caution because the Queen is not to be fooled. If you ever trusted me in the past, now you must do so more than ever. Do not see that woman. I fear for your safety. Protect yourself from her powers. You must trust me. You must. I leave you now with the promise that I will write again as soon as I can.

Yours,

Fairy Godmother

March 27

I will need to devise a plan for how to avoid the promise that I made to the Queen and the main reason for her agreeing to have me travel to France. Your words of warning concern me, and I wish we could speak our minds to each other so that I could better understand the reason behind your admonition. With your magic, you have helped me come very far, and I will not falter along the path. I will trust your counsel.

Earlier today Clarissa returned with wonderful news. She had visited her sick cousin, who is well again. She and I have spoken all through the long day about plans for France, and although the Queen has not spoken her mind to me about who will travel to Paris with me, I assume that my dearest Clarissa will be chosen to attend me, as we are often together and the best of friends.

I have told her my story of meeting with the Queen and of my promise to see the mysterious woman in France. Clarissa thinks that she might be a midwife who uses herbs and other natural remedies to aid women unable to bear children. I have remained silent about you. Clarissa and I are close friends, but I want to keep my relationship with you private for now. The secret that we share is a personal bond between us, and I desire to keep our correspondence solely between us, for now.

Clarissa is often judgmental, and I wish her not to color my fondness for you, as she would ask question upon question about why you were not by my side to help me. I can trust her, but I do not wish to reveal my thoughts to her yet. Rather, she and I talked about France and what might happen if I did drink the potions that the witch would give to me.

I have wanted to have a child for several years now. At first, I thought that a child would come naturally to the Prince and me, but that was not so. Becoming a mother would be good for me. I am young, and will be able to love and teach my child much. I will be able to be a good mother and give my children what I did not have when I was a growing up. Yet after a few years of trying and failing, I have come to face the truth. I may not be able to have children. I have talked to local nannies and tried all sorts of remedies, but none have worked. I have prayed, begged and hoped to be with child, but I am still childless. I fear that I am barren. I lost my mother at such a young age and had hoped that I would have a family of my own and that I could raise my children, loving them and showering them with my joy. I will not lie to you now, for I am tempted to see the witch and drink her potions because I long to have a child. However, I will not falter. I acknowledge your warning and will adhere to it.

Yet, if I am honest, I had hoped that a child would allow me to build a life away from the Prince. My entrance into motherhood would require me to take on new responsibilities, and I could ignore the Prince because raising our child would become my duty and day's work. I have longed for such responsibilities, for I tire of the endless balls.

Now I will soon go to Paris to find my destiny. The Queen wants me to visit a witch who will give me a fertility potion, whereas I wish to see the plays and hear the poems and take in the art of the city. If I visit not the witch, when you and I reunite, would you, with your magic help me to have a child?

I cannot see how my future will unfold, but I understand that what is about to be set in motion will change my life forever. I will be going down a path that I must travel. I feel called to go to Paris. I do not know how else to describe it, but I have an urgent voice inside me, deep within, that is telling me to go. I do not know why. I think that maybe some wanderlust plays tricks on me, and this trip will bring me some much needed joy. I will see what I have not. Taste life beyond what I have here, but also experience something of the world. I am concerned for the future. I cannot deny my fear. Good night.

April 8

Many days have passed, and I have heard nothing as to when our journey will begin. Yet, last night, the Prince returned from his travels. He came to see me, and I had the temptation to refuse him. He came into my room and sat himself down on a chair next to the window, leaning forward with his hands folded together.

"I wanted to speak with you about our last encounter." He coughed with nervousness and continued. "Let me be frank with you. I have treated you unkindly and I wish for you to forgive me."

He sounded contrite enough, but I doubted him. "May I ask the reason for your change of mood?"

"Mother asked that I come speak to you." He saw the frown on my face and held up his hand. "There is more to my reasoning. If we are to go to France together, I thought it best to reconcile with you."

"What would you have me say, as you have left me these long days?" I chanced upon the truth. "I am not so innocent to know that there are not others who have charmed you."

He stood up in a flash and came close to me. "Yes, I do not hide them. I have others whom I am close with, but so has every other member of court."

"What about us?" I had to know.

"Our union?" He chose his words with care. "You and I are to have children to keep my father's line strong."

He saw my lip tremble as I could not stop the emotion that had welled up within me. "But our love? What of that?"

"Of course, I still love you." He put his arm around me.

"But you love others, too?"

"Cinder, I am the Prince." He took his arm off of me and made to kiss me on the forehead, but I pulled away.

"When we met, you loved me. I know it for I saw the love in your eyes. What has happened?" I fought to withhold my tears. "Why have you abandoned me?"

He sighed and folded his arms across his chest. "You love so deeply and with such strength, whereas I am like the wind. I still love you. I do. Can we not reconcile and be happy again?"

"You give me no reason to believe you and ask for all, but give nothing back to me?" I backed away from him.

His anger begin to rise within as his neck turned splotchy. I had to tread with care. "You are a Princess, and before I married you what were you?"

"I know who I was before and who I am now. You need not treat me so. Have I not been a good wife to you?"

"I think you might decide to be less argumentative with me and be happy with your station."

My hands shook in frustration and anger. "Happy? You want me to be happy when I know that I am one of many? How can I be happy knowing that?"

"You can be happy with your station now, with the friends you have made and the life you now have."

He turned away from me, but I yelled at his back. "I want more. I want you to love me as you once did. I want to be remembered and cherished and not neglected and treated with disdain. I am your wife!"

The Prince spun around and rushed toward me. He grabbed me by my arms and held me still, his face only inches from my own. "Do you know why I married you? Do you?"

His grab on me hurt, and I tried to pull away. Seeing me flinch in pain, he loosened his hold and said, "I married you because of the magic, the glory of it all, and the wonder that you, in all the realm, were surrounded by power and light."

"I once loved you." I knew of no other words to contain my hurt.

"I loved the story of your Fairy Godmother and the glass slipper and seeing you in that magical dress that first night at the ball. I loved you because I thought you were different. But in the end, you are simply a rag girl dressed in fancy clothes."

His words bit deep and I slapped him across his face.

The shock on his face was plain to see, but then his anger exploded and a murderous rage broke out on his face. He came for me. But then, gaining control of himself, pushed past me, his body still tensed with rage. On his way to the door, he kicked a table over, smashing it to pieces. I could hear him rushing down the hall, and a silence fell over my bedroom. I wanted the tears to stop, but they did not.

When I retired to bed that night, I cried because I knew that my life had changed. The Prince and I could be no more. We would need to come to some resolution, and I did not know what that agreement would be, for my sorrow was too deep to consider the future. How he and I would reconcile before going to France, I do not know. I cannot write more, as I am too distraught.

April 10

There had been no news yet from the Queen about Paris or of the Prince and his whereabouts. I feared that he had headed off again on one of his excursions, drinking and whoring away his father's funds, but at breakfast today I spied him walking among the castle's grounds with two of his friends. I turned away because I did not wish him to think that I cared for him, as my anger is still bright and sharp.

Tonight I shall talk with Clarissa. We have not had a moment alone. I cannot write more now, as I must go.

April 11

What would I do without my constant and true friend? My dearest Clarissa, again, has calmed me. Last night she took me outside after dark and we walked the castle grounds until she found her destination. Tucked away in a far corner, nearly forgotten, she brought us to a small fountain surrounded by several stone benches to sit on. The water trickled slowly and soothed my nervousness, for I still felt ill at ease.

Clarissa took my hands in hers and asked me to tell her why I had been so upset. I told her about the Prince and his anger toward me, and the pain swelled up within as I told her that he had been brutally honest with me, confessing to the other women in his life. I cannot tell you the deep anger within me at knowing these trespasses against my love for him.

After I told my story, Clarissa leaned back against the stone wall and the two of us listened to the trickling of the fountain. "What will you do?"

The same question has been an ever-constant irritant to my thoughts that I cannot expel. The thought is strong, comes to me when I am weakest and my options appear so limited. "I will go to Paris."

"The Queen will help you. She wants you to have a grandchild."

"I know that she will take care of me, but to live with him and to raise a child that is his…" I let the thought trail off. In my hand, I held a pebble. I rubbed my thumb around its smoothness and took comfort in the repetitive act. I could try to soothe myself within by appearing calm without.

"I will always be your friend and supporter. Do not waste precious time thinking of him." Clarissa hugged me, and I did my best to feel happy.

"What am I going to do?" The words escaped my lips, and as the question could not be answered with certainty we left it there to be heard by any faeries.

We did not speak of much else that night, but sat by the fountain looking up at the sky, wondering at the moon and all the stars. I know you are far away and have done your best to reach me, but how will I overcome such obstacles? Before I become depressive, I will head off as I have much to do.

April 18

Good news has finally come to me today! After several weeks of waiting, I received notice that Clarissa and I should be prepared to leave on our journey in two days. The Queen's messenger said no more to me. When I told Clarissa the news, she shouted and clapped her hands as she admitted to me that she had hoped and prayed that she would come with me on my trip. After dinner, the Queen called both of us to her private chamber. She was dressed formally this time, and I acted with my best manners so that I could show thankfulness for her help.

She pointed down the hall and asked, "Do you know what the King and his men are doing tonight?"

I glanced at Clarissa and saw that neither of us did. "Your Majesty, we do not."

She took her crown off and threw it onto the table next to her. Only a few candles lit the room. The Queen took her wig off and gave it to a young attendant who came up behind her. "They plan their strategy in Egypt against Napoleon." She picked up a map on her desk and threw it onto the floor. "Our countries are at war, and the revolutionary spirit of America and France has the King frightened."

The Queen snapped her fingers, and another attendant came forward with a glass of wine. Clarissa and I remained still, unsure of what we should say.

Taking a sip of wine, the Queen swallowed, smiled and said, "While the men focus on war, we women must plan for life. Do you understand me?"

"Yes, Your Majesty." Clarissa and I said in unison.

"You both will be heading to the countryside for several months. At least that is what the court will be told." The Queen smiled and stood up, coming toward us. Both Clarissa and I curtsied low as she stopped in front of us. "Both of you rise and look at me!"

We followed her command and saw the fury in her face. "I tire of the world of men and their ineptitude. My son and his childish games, my husband and his wars, and a tiny despot in France who wants to rule the world." She touched my chin and pointed my face up toward heaven. "You both are going to Paris and will play the roles I have set for you. Do you understand me?"

I nodded with great emphasis.

She released my chin and said, "I have written to a friend, and we will visit the healer once a time can be arranged."

"Your Majesty, where will we be staying?" Clarissa asked.

"Outside of Paris at the Château de Malmaison with Joséphine de Beauharnais." The Queen waved over an attendant and pointed at us whispering a command. "I will arrange for my son and I to come visit as soon as I can find him. He has run off, no doubt causing great trouble. Once I have arrived, I will personally accompany you both to the healer."

Clarissa hazarded a quick look of concern at me, but I ignored her. The attendant handed us glasses of wine and we accepted.

"Let us have a toast, as I am merry that my plan has come to fruition." The Queen picked her glass up and raised it high. "To the future!"

I sipped the wine, as did Clarissa, and I longed to leave and return to my chamber. Having finished her glass of wine, the Queen sat back down. "The liberty I am granting you best be used wisely. Joséphine will show you both the wonders of Paris."

Clarissa smiled openly and curtsied low. "Thank you, Your Majesty."

I followed suit and curtsied low, but the Queen took me in with her gaze. "You will see your Paris and have your time of enjoyment with Joséphine and her friends. In return, you will return with me and produce an heir. Do you understand?"

"Yes, Your Majesty. I understand." I held her gaze and made her the promise.

She dismissed us shortly after this admonition, and both Clarissa and I were happy to go, for the Queen's will is not to be trifled with. Clarissa was excited with our secret travel to Paris and the world we were to be introduced to, but I felt caution in my heart as I would have time to think over my future. The Queen's actions were deliberate, and I realized that by being beholden to her I would need to follow through with my promise. She would personally see me to the witch and I suspect that she would orchestrate the path ahead, clearing all obstacles for me so that I could bear her a grandchild. How the witch can help me, barren as I am, would be magic indeed. My heart is unsettled, and I am now involved in events beyond my hopes to fully know. Let it be soon that we will be reunited. I pray that these words find you before the Queen forces me to see the witch. I am frightened, dear Fairy Godmother. Please hear me and help me. I go now, as I know not when I will have time to write next.

April 26

We arrived at the Château de Malmaison on the 24th of April. The journey was long, and complicated by a Spring storm that made crossing the channel difficult. We were in Dover for several days due to the rough seas and dangerous winds. The actual crossing only took a little under half a day. And the journey from Calais to the Château de Malmaison took less than a day's travel.

When Clarissa and I arrived, the Queen's attendants assisted us with our luggage, and six guards lined the sides of the path into the Château, receiving with great fanfare. Joséphine de Beauharnais and a host of her staff greeted us at the door of the Château. We were exhausted from our journey, and I remember only that Joséphine spoke quickly in French, welcoming us to her home. She introduced me to several people, but only a young man named Henri greeted us in English. He held a lute in his hand, having been practicing a song for our arrival, and he smiled at me, taking my hand as we passed through the front gate. Clarissa and I remained fairly quiet, thanking our hostess, and we were quickly taken to our rooms, with Henri waving after us, as we were cold and fatigued from the rain.

Later that night we had a grand dinner, and I soon learned that Joséphine enjoys displaying her wealth for her guests. The dinner consisted of more than several dozen guests, but both Clarissa and I feigned tiredness and retired to our rooms early so that we could talk and prepare ourselves for the weeks ahead. The Château is a work of beauty, with Joséphine renovating sections that had been damaged from the revolution. She informed us that she had purchased the Château a little more than a year ago, and the work continues through today. She hopes that one day she can add a greenhouse in the back and capture the beauty of all the French roses.

At dinner, to my right, sat Henri who entertained Clarissa and me throughout the meal with his tales of music and wonderment. His English skills are impressive. Most of the people we met speak only a few phrases. In the two days that we have been here, I have seen much to surprise me, but I find most of this society similar to that in England. I have been introduced to so many people that I cannot remember all their names. Joséphine is a wonderful host, sharing with us the latest on music and art. I have enjoyed my time thus far, but I do miss my room back at the castle. I will try my best to write and keep these pages filled, but I suspect that my free time will be limited.

April 29

Joséphine has been a kind and gentle hostess. She has given Clarissa and me time to ourselves rather than to thrust us into the busy days and nights of her home. Each night there have been dinner guests and music and dancing. As I am alone now in my room, I have asked Joséphine for more ink and paper so that I can write. She thinks that I am interested in poetry, and I find that suits me well, for I am cautious about my personal writing. I have hidden my journal in the hope that no one will find it. I do not lack trust of my hostess or of the attendants the Queen has generously lent us; I crave solitude to work and require an environment in which I can be assured that my thoughts are my own.

My mind has drifted to thinking of the Prince, and my thoughts are dark and clouded. I have imagined running away, leaving all I know, in the hope that I will be free of him and I can… Can what? Here is where my plans crumble into dust because I have no means of my own to do anything. I will not return to my father's house to be treated like a common servant girl. I have no letters of reference that I could use to find placement with a family to help raise children.

In time, soon I should think, Joséphine will come to me and ask when I wish to go to the witch. I will try to stall her, but I will need your help. If I run away, I have no means to sustain myself. Where would I go? I have time to think about my plan of action, but my choices are restricted to either following the Queen's plan or leaving on my own.

Please, will you help me?

Dear Cinderella,

How I wish I could simply wave my wand and rescue you from your plight! But I cannot do so as even my magic has limits. I ask of you to be patient and to trust me. I am a long way off, yet I am coming for you. Please, trust me.

Be wary of the witch, and if you are forced to see her before I arrive, you will need to question what she tells you. Listen to your innermost thoughts, and you will find the path to truth. When I return to you, I will aid you with all of my power. Enjoy your time at the Château, and I shall return as soon as I can. May light and beauty keep you safe until then.

Yours,

Faerie Godmother

May 1

Henri escorted Clarissa and me on a tour of the grounds, and we enjoyed a beautiful lunch outside today.

When we were walking, I asked him, "How do you know Joséphine?"

Clarissa elbowed me in the side for asking such a direct question, but with the beautiful sun and warm air I chanced an intimate question.

He smiled and replied, "You wonder if she is my mistress?"

I blushed as I had not thought that. "No, no, I did not mean to imply anything of the kind. Please, forgive me."

He took my hand and kissed it and bowed low. "There is nothing to forgive. You are simply being curious." He pointed to all the grounds and at the Château and said, "After the revolution and the terror, my family were no more. My title has been stripped and I have lost all of my lands and am now beholden to Joséphine's generosity."

Clarissa thought best to change the dour subject and asked, "We often see you carry a lute with you. Do you study music here?"

"Oui, I sing and have practiced now for the last years, learning a few instruments, but my favorite is the lute." He mimicked playing one in his hands. "I enjoy the feel of the lute as I strum the strings, and the beauty of its sound."

"Will you play for us one day soon?" I asked him, for I enjoyed his company and his demeanor.

"For our most wonderful guests from across the water, I will gladly play for you." He reached out and took my hand, pulling me with him as he started to run. "But first, I must show you these wonderful gardens." Clarissa and I ran will him and we laughed and had such an enjoyable afternoon that, dare I say, I forgot my troubles for some time.

Henri's enthusiasm for life is so fresh and new that I find myself enjoying his company. It is helping me become settled here in France. I look forward to the next few weeks, as this freedom that I now have has been most welcome, and I would like to experience even more of it.

May 4

Last night Joséphine, some of her close friends, Clarissa, Henri and I went to Paris for the first time, to attend the Opera. Paris at night is beautiful to behold, with such wonderful people to see. I have seen such wonder and light, but the music at the Opera was most beautiful. We saw a piece by Cherubini entitled Médée. I sat next to Clarissa, and together we looked peered down upon all the women and men in the audience, dressed so magnificently. We were both so happy. Our dream had come true. We had finally arrived in Paris, and on such a wonderful warm night. Henri sat on my right, for we have become fast friends, and he kept whispering to me throughout the opera, translating parts that my weak language skills could not comprehend. Joséphine played her part well, and we were introduced as her cousins who had fled to England during the revolution.

At the finale of the opera, I sat in awe of the music and singing, yet I could not turn away from Henri. His face held such emotion, and I could see the tears in his eyes as he watched Médée stand with the blood-stained knife in her hand, having slain her own children. My heart went out to him as he watched Médée enter the temple that was engulfed in flames. Henri's face contorted in anguish and he reached out for my hand. He squeezed my flesh with such firmness but did not turn his gaze from the stage. The opera ended, and we waited for some time to gather our composure. Henri, most affected, patted my hand and then pulled his hand away. After the opera, our carriage took us back to the Château, and we dined well.

I have enjoyed my time here and have often forgotten why I have come, as my days are filled with music, laughter and life. At night, Joséphine has such lavish parties that I am amazed by their expense, but I have seen such before back home. I will continue to enjoy my time here, but I pray that you come to me soon. Joséphine has not mentioned seeing the witch, and I am resolved to not mention the topic. I know that soon my luck will change, but not today.

May 12

Last night Joséphine invited her friends from Paris to a masquerade ball. The dancing and revelry went on until the early morning hours, yet I had become bored of the music and drinking soon after midnight. Clarissa decided to retire to bed, but I wanted to take a walk outside in the garden as the night was clear and warm.

I walked through the gardens, and I came out to an open field from which I could view the Château in all its majesty. Running quickly across the field, I could see a fox rushing into a flower bed, its tail bushy and bright. The low moon lit the grounds, and I could hear far-off shrieks of delight as people chased each other through the rose gardens. I continued walking and heard a beautiful sound from a lute. I guessed who would be playing and chanced to quietly walk until I found him. Alone and sitting by a fountain sat Henri with his lute across his lap.

He wore white, which suited him well in the warm spring night. I watched him, listened to him play, and then he sang. I did not understand all of the words because my French is still minimal, but his voice echoed the sentiments of deep longing. At the end of the song, he was quiet, looking up at the stars and asked, "Did you like?"

Startled a bit as I did not think he had seen me, I recovered quickly and replied, "Yes, I did." I moved closer to him and leaned against a low garden wall. "Why are you not joining in the revelry?"

I could see that he had prepared his response, choosing his words carefully, watching me intently. "I do not wish to play such games tonight."

I nodded and let the conversation drift away, staring up at the stars with him, trying to take in the night.

"May I ask you a question?" A crooked smile broke out across his face.

"If I say, 'no,' will you take that question back?"

He chuckled and waited, unsure as to how I would respond.

"Yes, you may." I wondered what he would ask, and maybe it was the few glasses of wine I had had, but…

"Why have you come here?" He stood up, leaving the lute on the ground, and closed the distance between us. He stood next to me, careful not to touch my dress, but close enough that he could see my face in the moonlight. He watched, waiting.

I wondered if he tested me to see how I would answer. "I came here to renew myself." I thought the answer vague enough that I did not lie, yet withheld the full truth.

"I hear that you have come here to be free of your husband for a while." He picked up a pebble and flicked it toward the fountain. "Is this true?"

I chanced to tell the truth. "Yes, that is part of the reason."

He leaned toward me and spoke low. "I see." Reaching for another pebble, he rolled it across the palm of his hand.

We stood there next to each other listening to the fountain and the far off yells and laughter from the guests.

"You seem unhappy tonight. Is that so?"

I again spoke the truth. "Yes, I am unhappy. I worry about my future."

"It saddens me to hear that." He flicked another pebble into the fountain. "I have an idea that will bring laughter to you. Will you come with me?" His smile was true and open.

I observed him, wondering what Clarissa would do, and then realized that the Prince could not see me because he was in England. I would take a chance with Henri and trust him. "Yes, I will come with you." I stopped and added, "I simply wish to walk with you."

"Oui, of course." He grabbed my hand and pulled me away from the fountain. "Allez! Come."

We ran through the gardens and headed to a small pond behind the back of the Château. The moonlight reflected off the water, and Henri pointed at a small structure. "Voilà!"

"Where are we?"

"Joséphine has named it the Temple of Love. Come see."

We rushed over to the circular structure, which resembled a stone gazebo. In the center, a statue of Cupid stood tall, with wings outstretched behind him. Henri sat on the edge of the structure, near the water. He pointed up at the moon and out at the water and asked, "How can you stay unhappy with such beauty before your eyes?"

I laughed and sat next to him in wonder at the beautiful sight.

He hummed to himself for a few moments and then became quiet, turning pensive. "I have come here often, for my heart soars to great heights and here I can forget my troubles and be free for a while."

"You are right to come here. It is beautiful." I heard the crickets chirping in the brush below. "Thank you for bringing me here."

"When we have more time, I will take you and your friend here and we will have fun that day. I promise."

Before I could reply, a large frog jumped into the water and, startled, I screamed.

Henri laughed and mimicked the frog's croaking. I laughed at my foolishness, as well.

He came close to me and croaked in my ear, and I pushed him away. We both laughed, and then he leaned in again and kissed me. His taste was warm and full, with a hint of mint. I kissed him back, and I did not think. His love for me poured out of him like the milky way, and I drank of his goodness, and his light filled me with such happiness. Is this what I had missed all these years?

Later, he could see me becoming sleepy and we returned to the Château. Once in my room, I looked out the window and smiled up at the moon. I have had a delicious evening of fun, and I pray that this time shall continue. Henri has impressed upon me his honesty and such strong gentleman qualities. Such traits in a man are rare I should think.

Good night, my Fairy Godmother, and may I see you soon.

May 14

As is usual after a big ball, yesterday was a quiet and reserved day. Many of the guests did not go to sleep until after the sun had risen. In fact, I did not see Joséphine until near dinner, and I suspect she was recovering from the night's festivities. I decided to go for a walk on my own, telling Clarissa that I had much thinking to do. I am tired of the dinners, the balls, and the endless events of extravagance that occur here. Joséphine has been a wonderful host, but my personal tastes are for calmer and more intellectual pursuits.

You must wonder what I think about Henri, for I have mentioned him often, and I suspect that soon Clarissa will ask me the same question. She has seen us talking alone, and she knows that in the years I have been married I have not taken to male companionship. Yet I am lonely, and my future stretches out before me in such confusion that I do not know what to do. I am attracted to Henri and am impressed with his charm and restraint.

I have been lonely for many months now, and it has been refreshing to laugh with both Clarissa and Henri as we explore the grounds of the Château. For now, I will be myself and simply enjoy my time.

I have a greater problem, though, which I am unsure how to solve. I do not know what to do because I have come to France for one reason and one reason only: To go to the witch to find a cure for being barren. I promised the Queen that I will do this for her, and she made the arrangements that allowed me to come here.

And I do not wish to go to the witch. But … .

For the last few weeks, I have had time to think about my relationship with the Prince and how it has changed so dramatically. How can I go to the witch and say that I want to have a child—with him? I do not want that at all. I wish to heed your warning about visiting her, yet a new thought has come to me. Do I not owe it to myself to go to the witch, talk with her, and find out if I can have children? I might not want to have a child with the Prince, but what about my future? Visiting her may not be the worst decision I could make, for I could then decide whether I wish to take the medicine to help me or not.

I will need to make a decision soon because I suspect that the Queen will arrive with her son to take us to the witch before the month is out. If I decline to go, I will face the Queen's wrath. She will turn on me, and all support I have from her will vanish. I do not know what my fate would be if I were cast out of the royal family, for I would have no place at all to live.

I am certain about one fact. I have decided that I will not have a child with the Prince. His behavior has been brutal, and he has made no attempt to change or even apologize. I suspect that the Queen has waited to come because, knowing her son's ways, she wishes me to have some peace of mind, if even for a short time. Yet yesterday on my walk a thought entered my mind, took root, and now I am decided. I wish no longer to be with the Prince. As a woman, I know that I do not have any rights or powers to separate myself from him. I cannot ask for a divorce, as I would not be heard. Only the King or the Prince can grant such a separation. We women raise the children and help keep stability in the home, but we have no voice in certain matters.

I have had much anger in me as of late because of my lack of power to control my own fate. Yet I am realizing that any power I may have now, or gain in the future, comes with choice, and having a choice is itself a very special form of power. I am choosing not to be with the Prince. He cannot change my mind, nor can his mother. If I am not with him, then I also will not be able to give birth to the heir. Without an heir, there is no line of succession to the throne. I may lack the political power to divorce him, but I can choose not to have his child. My logic assumes that the witch can help me with my problem. If she cannot, well, then the choice will be simple. The Queen will force the Prince to divorce me, as I will officially be declared barren and tossed aside. I do not quite know what would become of me. Would I be allowed to still live on the palace grounds and be taken care of? I suspect that they would not be so cold as to cast me out. It would be a sad life that I would lead there, but without a way to sustain myself I might have worse.

But what if I am not declared barren but refuse to bear the Prince's child? I will be obstructing the Queen's wishes, and I do not know how I would then be treated. I would need your help if I am abandoned. Would you help me?

There is no one at the Château right now but me, and inside my heart I know this: I want to be loved, I deserve to be happy, and I will move forward to find a way to change my life. If I am no longer a Princess and am disgraced, then so be it. I am tired of living my life with the Prince. With freedom in my heart, I can admit that now. I know opportunities will come to me, but I am unable to see that far in the future. I can only discern the few steps in front of me along the path I am choosing to pursue.

A walk through the Château's grounds has helped calm my mind and allowed me to make some important decisions. I am rather proud of the progress I have made. If you can read these words, please reply, for your comfort and assurance would help ease my mind. I need to go now as I am being called.

May 23

Dear Cinderella,

Your words are so precious to me and I wish I could be at your side to help you with your difficult decisions. Soon, soon I will be with you! I can see the path now, and the road is not too long.

In all the years I have aided and advised young women, I have told them to follow their hearts. You are young, and the Prince lacks respect for you. Yet Henri is a man of honor and displays concern and trust. You would do well to befriend him, as in your new life he could assist you.

I had hoped that our magic bond would be stronger and that through our writings we would be brought together sooner, yet that is not to be. My magic flies on the wind and grows stronger each day, but you will need to protect yourself. With the limited power of sight that I possess, you are most correct that soon the Queen will come to take you to the witch. I had hoped that you could avoid that confrontation as her powers are strong. Use your newly found strength and listen to her words for she is full of guile. Be wary of her.

Now I must leave you again as my connection with you fades. My heart is with you and soon we will be together again. Use what you have learned to love. Allow your mind and heart to be open to possibility and the road will become clear.

Yours,

The Faerie Godmother

May 27

I am thankful for your words. They console me. When I am doubting, I run my fingers over your words and am happy to know that your magic is real. My time with Henri has been friendly and filled with much enjoyment. We have spent many long hours together, laughing and being outside in the glorious warm May sun.

Last night Clarissa came to see me. We had not seen each other since the day before, and she asked, "Have you decided what you will do when the Queen comes?"

Never one to obfuscate, she is direct. "I have made my decision."

Her hands twirled a necklace she wore, a sign that she was agitated with me. "And Henri, how does he fit into these plans?"

"I have not factored him into my plans." I had been working on my diary so I closed it and asked, "Why do you ask?"

"We have been friends for more than three years, have we not?"

"There is no matter to be concerned with, if that is what you ask." I tried to avoid the conversation, but Clarissa was not so easily dissuaded.

"The talk among the guests here is nothing but whisperings of your bond with Henri. Do you not see?"

I did not wish to be confronted in such a matter, and Clarissa's words angered me. "Have I not suffered in my marriage enough that I cannot enjoy the company of a friend?" I leaned closer to her and lowered my voice. "When my husband parades himself to all the women he desires, leaving me at home to play the role of the good Princess? I will have none of it anymore."

"Will you not heed my advice?" Clarissa reached for my hand, but I pulled away. "Henri is young and attractive, and there is great charm in him, but you are not a man, and if you fall, the Queen, if she learns of your fondness, will be unforgiving."

"Have we not known each other long enough, and you come here to threaten me?" My color rose and my hands began to shake in anger. "You would go the Queen and speak lies to her to destroy my name? Is that what you speak?"

"Please, listen to me." She implored with her hands. "I would not betray you, but there are others here that watch and listen. Joséphine's friend Isabella has the look of one who would gladly betray any confidences to help bring disorder to the world. She is not to be trusted."

I agreed with Clarissa's assessment, but I did not wish to listen as my anger had taken hold of me. "I have come to France to learn of art, poetry, and the enjoyment of life and all it has to offer. Henri is a beautiful friend and his heart is true."

"That may be so, but we have only known him for a month's time." She quieted as our attendants came into the room to light the candles. Darkness had begun to descend in my room. "I urge you to have patience."

I waited until the attendant had finished his work, and then I stood up and poured myself a glass of wine. I did not offer Clarissa any. "Why do you say all of this to me now?"

"I am your friend, and I wish to help protect you."

"Is there not more to this?" My left hand itched and I felt it burn with my anger. I had not been so angry in a long time. "Maybe you seek Henri's eye and try to cast me aside?"

Clarissa remained quiet.

"Do I speak the truth, and now you have no words?" I put my glass down and asked again, "Have I reached the heart of the matter?"

Clarissa spoke low and folded her hands in her lap. "Do you know how difficult it is to be your friend, you, who lights up every room, and draws men to her like moths to a flame? I am always unnoticed yet I am constant and true."

For a moment, my anger deflated and I listened.

"You came to court and swept through the castle becoming beloved and winning the heart of the Prince. But now here in France, married though that you are, I chance upon a young, handsome man and again you sweep in and steal his affections so that he can see none but you."

"There are other men and I am stealing no one from anyone. Henri enjoys my company."

"Yes, he does, and I have not interfered with your enjoyment of his company. Yet I am your friend, and as such, it is in my nature to speak my mind to you. I am concerned for your well-being and ask you to have patience in this matter."

"Why, so that you can win Henri's affections?" Even to me, my words sounded coarse and hurtful.

"No, that is not my intention." Clarissa stood up and curtsied to me. "You know what is right, I am most sure. I have spoken my words to you, and now you must decide what is best for you. Good night."

She left before I could find the appropriate words to retort. The spitefulness in my words worried me. I do not care what anyone says about my time with Henri. I enjoy his company and will continue to do so, following my heart. How long has it been since I have laughed and enjoyed my time? I do not remember the last time that the Prince and I walked together and talked without tension and bitter words between us. Now is my time, and I will allow myself to feel because I have been denied for too long. I am happy to spend my days with Henri, listening to music and walking the grounds.

Clarissa has angered me, and I need time to think, for I am not calm. I will go for a walk now and write when I am more at ease.

May 30

I have had several quiet days of intense enjoyment with Henri. He and I have talked much about poetry and art and philosophy, and my mind has opened and become aware of all of our Creator's beauty. I feel I have awoken from a long, deep sleep. My time with Henri is most enjoyable. Each day, we start off with breakfast, and then pack some food and walk the grounds, and we only stop to rest for lunch at the Temple of Love.

I cannot put into words how I feel. My mind is clear and my heart is full with such emotion. I am renewed and vibrant with life, and my imagination is filled with joy and the potential for a life that will be filled with great and tender love. In my heart, I am a married woman no more, for I have decided my path. I do not know the way nor do I know of Henri's true feelings toward me, but it is clear that our connection is complete, whole and true. How is it possible that two minds can be so open and accepting of each other? This natural flow of conversation between us is truly heaven sent.

Today Henri and I sat by the pond at the Temple of Love and he asked, "If you were not a Princess, what would you like to do in life?"

A good question, without doubt. I looked at him as he spread cheese on a piece of crusty bread and watched his hands. "I would be a writer telling my story to the world."

He passed me the piece of bread and I accepted. "Such a scandalous profession you choose! Would you not be best served by being attendant to your house and following the will of your husband?"

He laughed and I broke off a piece of bread and threw it at him. He avoided my projectile and continued laughing. "Dear Sir, I do not find your words to be amusing."

"But Madame," he stood and bowed low, "I am only stating the truth that your place is clearly defined and set according to the rules of society. Is this not so?" He loved to mock me.

"I suppose you can say it is." I looked out at the water and my heart burst forth. "But need it be so? What if I could write as a man and have my books published like Wordsworth or Coleridge?" I stopped and my left-hand suddenly ached as though needles and pins had burst out through all of my fingers. I took my weight off my hand and said, "With their vision and words, they create such wonderful poetry, and why can I not do the same with my words?"

Henri knelt down in front of me and came close. Less than a hand's span from my lips, he asked, "Yes, why not?"

He smirked and then jumped backwards, nearly knocking over his cup of wine.

I said little after that. I looked at the swans on the pond and listened to the insects buzzing through the air. A moment of intense feeling washed over me and, dear Fairy Godmother, for a moment I imagined my future as a writer, and my heart soared with such pleasure.

Henri cut a piece of ham and snickered at me. He knew he had won our argument.

Only I impeded myself from becoming what I most wanted. If France and America could overthrow their Kings, why could I not do as I wished?

"Princess?" He leaned close to me and poured me some more wine.

I smiled at him and asked, "Yes, dear Sir?"

"For me, you can be anything you like, and I would still treasure our friendship." His French accent was thick and true.

My heart went out to him then and he clinked his cup against mine and we drank.

The rest of the afternoon went well, and now I sit alone by candlelight, writing. I have not spoken to Clarissa in days. I think it best that our tempers cool before we say more hurtful words to each other. Yet my mind is not on her. It is fixed on Henri. He is everything that the Prince is not. I will not waste time thinking of my husband, and yet, I feel some guilt at my actions. I shall not lie.

How I wish you were here to advise me on my course of action with Henri! I will to bed now, as I hope to rest and let my mind be at ease.

June 5

The Queen will arrive tonight. Joséphine invited me to a late morning breakfast, and I broke off an engagement with Henri to attend. We sat in the shade of the Château looking out at the beautiful garden. She held in her hand a letter with the royal seal on it and said, "Your Queen and her guests will arrive this evening. Her Majesty has informed me that she wishes for you to prepare for her arrival and that soon you should travel to complete your business here."

She put the letter down and watched me for my response.

Careful not to betray much emotion, I replied, "It is good news that you bring and I will prepare myself for her and her son's arrival."

"And what of Henri?" She folded her hands in her lap. "What will you do about him?"

I remained quiet and held my heart still.

"May you know it and we be clear together—I am your ally and will assist you if need be."

Her words washed over and relief settled into my heart. "Thank you for your help." I could barely whisper, as my heart was full and I did not know how to put to words my feelings.

"Why not go and enjoy this beautiful day with him?" She stood up and curtsied and left me.

I spent the rest of the day with Henri and we talked, but he had no concerns about the impending arrival of the Queen and of my husband. He tried to lighten my mood, but I had difficulty relaxing as I was fearful of what would happen. He and I had an early dinner and spent the end of the day watching the sun set as we sat in our Temple of Love. The Queen will arrive within the next few hours and I wait with a heavy heart.

June 6

The Queen, the Prince, several of her personal attendants, and six guards arrived late last night. They had all pretended to be lesser nobles visiting from England to decrease interest in the strained relations between our two countries. Having never stopped on the road, their plain carriage proceeded directly from Calais to the Château. Where the King of England thought the Queen visited, I do not know. As for the Prince, he would keep quiet about their location in exchange for his mother's overlooking some of his misdeeds. I found the relationship between Joséphine and the Queen of interest, as they were not friends but had a certain respect for each other.

When I went to attend to the Queen's arrival, I saw Clarissa for the first time in days. She came to stand by me and reached out to gently squeeze my hand. I returned the gesture, and we waited until the carriage pulled up and the guards disembarked from their horses. When the carriage door opened, the Prince stepped down and walked forward to stand before me. He smiled and put his hand out to me. In deference, I curtsied low and said, "Welcome, my dear husband."

He stood next to me, and I longed to see Henri in the crowd. To see his face would give me strength and support, but he was not present. The Prince remained quiet, and we waited as two of the Queen's attendants helped her exit the carriage. She wore a plain dress and appeared less regal than I had ever seen her. Joséphine curtsied low, as did all the women, and the Prince bowed lightly to his mother.

She and Joséphine exchanged a few words and then the Queen approached me. I remained curtsied and waited.

"You may rise." She leaned close to me and said, "I do hope you have enjoyed your time here."

I averted my eyes as was due her station and replied, "Joséphine has been an excellent hostess and I have thoroughly enjoyed my stay."

"Tomorrow morning you and my son will attend me and we will discuss when we are visiting the witch." The Prince stiffened next to me but remained quiet. "I would like to finish our business here soon, as I have matters to attend to at home."

She walked on with Joséphine trailing behind her, and the gathering slowly scattered. The Prince quickly hastened to leave my side. "I will see you in the morning."

I mumbled a response, but he had already left with one of the Queen's attendants. Clarissa came beside me again and asked, "Would you like to share some tea?"

I agreed, and we spent time healing the breach in our friendship. But my mind was on Henri. I looked for him in all the faces we passed. I suspect he would rather avoid the trouble of the arrival as he would not be missed. I wished that I could do the same. Our stay here is solely dictated by Joséphine and the Queen. There are rumors that the First Consul is consolidating his power and will declare himself Emperor. Joséphine does not often talk about him because he is in Egypt. I admire the power of these two women. They have found a means to circumvent the wishes of two of the most powerful men in Europe.

I went to bed soon after, and today I meet with the Queen and the Prince. My fate will be decided, and I fear that my strength slips away. I do not know what I will say. Where is Henri when I need him? I wish to see him, but I have looked for him and been told that he is not at the Château. I must go. I need to prepare myself.

June 7

I have returned from meeting with the Queen and her son. Tomorrow we see the witch in Paris. When I was allowed entry into the Queen's private chamber, I curtsied low and saw the Prince sitting in a chair by the window. He did not turn to me or give me greeting, but rather appeared to be occupied by thoughts on his mind.

I maintained my curtsy and spoke as I was obliged. "Your Majesty."

The Queen snapped an order, and her attendants left the room. She sat down on her chair, brought from England, as I recognized its gold intricate design. "Rise."

I stood and averted my gaze away from both mother and son.

"I have spoken to my son about his indiscretions and he has informed me that he promises to halt such activities and reconcile with you during the next year." She stood and walked over to the Prince and laid her hand on his shoulder. "Is this not true?"

The Prince turned to me, his face absent of emotion. "We have discussed the matter and I have so agreed."

She smiled and I remained frozen in place.

"What would you have of me, Your Majesty?"

The Queen removed her hand from her son's shoulder and came toward me. "Tomorrow, we three will visit the Parisian woman who will offer you a remedy that will allow you to give birth to the future heir to the throne. Will you come freely?"

"Yes, of course." I did not hesitate to answer.

She took my hand and pulled me closer to her son. "There is much strife in the world with men causing wars and revolutions. Yet there is always hope in times when women come forth to be strong. Is that not so?"

Neither of us was certain whom she spoke to, so we both remained silent. As she turned her attention away, the Prince looked up at his mother and asked, "How long do you expect to be able to control us? Revolution is forever sparking in people's hearts these days."

He stood and pulled away from her. "Father would be interested to hear of our secret journey to France, would he not?"

The Queen was silent, and I felt a slight increase in pressure from her hand to mine. I, too, stayed quiet, pretending that I could be a mouse.

"Will your words against me never cease after all I have done for you?" She spat the words at him.

"Mother, your kindness knows no bounds as we can all attest." His sarcastic comment hung heavy. "Yet I grow weary of you and of your interference."

The Queen released my hand and faced him. "How would you secure monies if I were to have you cut off?" She paced around the chair that he stood by like a lioness. "Would your so-called friends stand by you if you were not paying for their drinking bills?"

The Prince opened his mouth to speak and, with great effort, he remained quiet.

The Queen nodded and smiled. "We can help each other if we make an effort to do so. Will we all be in agreement, or shall we continue our argument?"

She glanced at me for support. My moment to rebel had passed, and I said, "I will come with you tomorrow of my own will so that the Prince and I could reconcile."

I did not speak any great words of intensity and feeling. I remained subservient and enveloped by fear of the Queen's wrath.

The Queen put her arm out to me and bade me take her hand. I did so and came toward her as she pulled me close. She then reached out to her son and waited for him to take her other hand.

"Come to us and we will put aside all this disagreement." She stood firm, waiting, arm outstretched. "Our agreement will not last forever, as the two of you can come to a different understanding once she is with child."

The Prince stood firm with arms crossed over his chest. "What I do, I do for father. Remember, that." He took her hand, and she pulled him toward me.

"Of course, do we not all act so that the King may stay strong and his line will endure?"

She placed our hands together and then stepped back. Together he and I stood joined, and I remembered our marriage day in the cathedral. Had we come so far to be standing now before his mother, obviously strained to be together?

The Queen glided to her chair and sat smiling at the alliance she had formed between us. "Thank you. Now I would recommend that you both separate and spend the night apart so that you each can have some rest for tomorrow."

I curtsied low, released the Prince's hand and backed out of the room. My heart beat wildly as I left, and I kept my eyes averted to the ground. I stumbled back to my room upset and needing to speak with a friend. I do not know what to do except to remain in obedience and, for that, I feel trapped.

The hour is late and I am to sleep now for tomorrow I will need my strength and wits about me. If I rise early enough, perchance I might find Henri or Clarissa to speak with before I am forced to leave for the journey.

Oh, dear Fairy Godmother, the hour is late and dark. I pray I have made the right choice.

June 8

In a few hours, we see the witch. I have learned that she lives in a small home in the center of Paris near the river. The Queen, Prince and I will take a carriage there, and I am nervous and am unsure as to what I can expect in meeting her.

Yet before I leave, I want to write that Joséphine visited me earlier this morning. After an early breakfast, I went to my room and then wanted to go for a walk outside through the gardens, hoping to find Henri.

As I walked toward the door of the Château, Joséphine came toward me as though she had been waiting for me to leave my rooms. She was alone, not attended by her friends.

Joséphine curtsied to me and asked, "Might I join you on your morning walk?"

"Bien sûr." I practiced my French and she smiled.

"Your French skills are becoming better a little each day."

We strolled through the garden, watching workers tend to the flowers and trim the large bushes. "I hope to one day speak with assurance."

Joséphine glanced around her to ensure we were truly alone and asked, "Do you wish to visit the witch today?" Her directness caught me off guard.

I kept quiet, thinking.

"If I intrude on you too much, I will remain silent." She took the path, heading to the Temple of Love. "But if not, I will help you."

I was surprised by her concern, but happy for her offer. "I am nervous and unsure what will happen at the witch's, but I do wish to visit her."

"I am glad to hear that." Joséphine adjusted her hair and spoke lower. "The Queen is one not to anger."

"We are in agreement."

Joséphine pointed at the Temple of Love ahead. "I had that built to remind me of my youth." She sighed. "All my thoughts of past love and what has become of it now." She turned to look at me. "Did you know that I was married before but my husband was guillotined during the Terror?"

"I did not know. I am so sorry to hear of your loss."

Joséphine patted me on my arm. "That was nearly 10 years ago. They imprisoned me during my husband's trial, and I feared that I would lose all that we had. After they killed Alexandre, I needed to find a way to survive and keep my two children."

I listened but did not know how to respond to such tragedy.

"I became the mistress of several prominent men in Paris and then I met Napoleon and we soon married."

"I had wondered how you met General Napoleon." I realized my rudeness and added, "I apologize for my bluntness. I meant no offense."

"And I take none. You are simply curious."

Joséphine walked into the temple and stood by the statue of cupid, looking out at the pond. "We are women and we will do what we need to survive. Do you not agree?"

"I am learning." I watched the swans out on the pond and wished Henri was here.

She broke the uncomfortable silence and asked, "Do you know my real name?"

"Is it not Joséphine?" I wondered out loud.

"My name is Rose but Napoleon has never liked it. He prefers my middle name, Joséphe, and started calling me Joséphine."

"Rose is such a pretty name." I remained lost in my thoughts.

Joséphine pulled a piece of crusty bread from a pocket and broke off a piece to feed to the swans. "Cinderella, what is your true name?"

For a moment, I had forgotten, as so many people called me by that name. She handed me a piece of bread and I flicked it to the birds. "My name is Sophia."

"Ah, the Goddess of Wisdom. Such a beautiful name."

I brushed the crumbs off of my hands and said, "I have not used my name in many years."

"Neither have I." She sat down near the pond and shielded her eyes from the bright, morning sun. "And the man who changed my name is off at war. I am here with money, extravagant parties and plenty to do, and men to keep me busy, but I will tell you a secret." She turned toward me and whispered conspiratorially, "I am not happy."

She was quiet for a moment and started to talk but then stopped. I could see that she was working hard on choosing the correct words. "I made my choices for my children and for my future. I had been in prison and had feared for my life. For me, I wanted to live, so I made myself available to those men in power. Yet I am not happy."

She gently touched my hand and then stood up. "I see that you are not happy. I pray you find a different path than I."

She said nothing else and walked away. I did not say much nor did she offer me a chance to respond. She was gone, but I sat thinking about all the wealth, power and luxury at her disposal. None of it mattered to her.

My opinion of Joséphine had changed much from our conversation, as I had thought her most interested in extravagance yet she had told me otherwise. Let me end here. I hope to find Clarissa or Henri before the Queen calls me to attend her.

June 8 near midnight

I am most miserable. Most of the day I wore wet clothes, as a heavy rain accompanied us to Paris, so I am cold. Yet I wanted to set this all down before I forget. We are back from the witch, and she refused to see us. The witch defied the Queen, her guards and all of her wrath, but still we were not allowed admittance to her home. Up until the last moment, I did not know who would go on this journey with me, but in the end it was the Queen, her son, her attendants, and six guards. The Queen had hand-picked those to come with us, and I should have known that the day would be filled with disappointment as the rain would not stop. It rained and turned cold. The wind blew the rain sideways at times, and we faced becoming wet each time we had to leave the carriage. The men on their horses must have been bitterly uncomfortable in such weather. I had hoped that Clarissa would come on the journey with us, but that was not to be. She did see us off, waving to me as we pulled away. I hoped to see Henri and to talk with him before I left, yet he did not show himself to us. I do not know where he is or when he will return.

We set off to the witch's, which was in a crowded section of Paris. Apart from the weather, the ride over was quiet enough. We all kept mostly to ourselves, watching the rain and the thick mud on the road. When we arrived at the house, I was a bit surprised because I had expected the witch to live alone in the countryside, thinking she lived in a small hut, near an overgrown garden, filled with herbs that she used for her potions. Yet her home was a small house near the Seine, the streets so narrow that our carriage forced others to the side of the street.

When we arrived, I remained calm, knowing that becoming nervous would not help me at all. I sat with my arms folded, wondering what would happen, focusing on the fact that this was only the first step along a difficult road. I saw the Queen's men-at-arms announce our arrival at the door, and they were refused entry.

The Captain came back, in the driving rain, and opened the carriage door and then kneeled in the mud. The rain streamed down him and he delivered the message.

"Your Majesty, the witch has asked me to inform you that we are to return on June 17th during the day of the full moon." He swallowed and continued, "She declines to see you today."

He bowed his head low, refusing to show his face.

Even I flinched in surprise and quickly glanced over to the Queen, trying to gauge her reaction. For her part, she remained calm, but her steely response frightened me. "Tell the witch that we will see her now!"

Looking uncomfortable, the Captain rose from the mud and headed back to the witch's home. I wrapped my blanket closer around me and kept my eyes down. I did not wish to make eye contact with the Queen. I could sense her anger, boiling up, and I did not want to give her any cause to direct it at me.

In a few minutes, the Captain returned again. He knelt in the mud and shook his head and said, "Your Majesty, she still refuses. Would you like us to use force?"

With great patience, he waited for the Queen's response and he soon received it. "Break down the door. We wish to enter immediately."

The Queen's attendants helped us out of the carriage and we stood with our parasols over us, but the mud soaked our feet and the rain could not be stopped. People looked out their windows at us, most likely wondering who we were and what trouble we were causing. The Captain banged on the witch's door with his armored fist and shouted to her, demanding that the door be opened. On the third time, he tried to break the door and failed, falling back without damaging the door at all. Two other guards tried to break the door, running full into it with their armored shoulders, and also failed. In the rain, for the next quarter of an hour, they tried using weapons, clubs, and, most creatively, a log to smash the door down, yet all attempts failed. They tried to break through the small window that had been shuttered, but again, to no avail.

We stood in the rain and waited. I glanced over at the Prince and he looked concerned, wondering why the door or window could not be broken. He avoided looking at me, but I could see him curious. After another quarter of an hour, the Captain of the guard returned to the Queen. His face was red, and he was out of breath. He knelt in the mud before her and said, "Your Majesty, I am sorry but we cannot win purchase on the door. Some magic protects it."

He lowered his head and waited. Imagining the Queen could use magic herself, I half expected her to conjure up a hellfire to burn the door down, but, alas, she had no such power. She stormed past the Captain and to the small house. She touched the door, and from inside a woman, hard to tell if she were young or old, said, "Listen to me well. I will not see you today. Return on the 17th of June during the full moon, but leave now and go get dry as you are not welcome today."

The Queen stopped short, removed her hand from the door and shouted back, "I demand to see you. Open this door and attend me!"

To our amazement, the door opened. Fearless, the Queen entered and we moved closer to see inside. But she came out after only a few minutes, her face angry. Clenched in her hand was a rolled up scroll.

She came up to me and thrust the scroll at me. "Read it. Read it now!"

Confused, I grabbed the scroll from her and saw that a tag had my name on it. I stammered some nonsense response and the Queen bit back, "I tried to open it and cannot do so. Open it now!"

I pulled at the tag and the red silk tie came away, and I unrolled the scroll. On it, only one line of text. I read it aloud unsure of what to make of it. "The heart has its reasons which Reason knows not."

The Queen grabbed the scroll from my hand, looking at both sides and then gave it back to me. She turned and rushed to the carriage. The Prince followed closely next to her and asked, "Mother, what did you see inside?"

She stopped, standing in the rain with no parasol, and said, "Nothing was inside. No furniture, clothing, or instruments of any kind. I only found the scroll in the center of the room."

We followed her back inside the carriage and the Queen ordered that we return to the Château with much haste. The men-at-arms mounted their horses and we were off. The Prince and I exchanged glances on the way back, but we remained quiet. The Queen closed her eyes and feigned sleep, but I could see her eyes twitching. I do not think I had ever seen her so angry and so powerless before. There was nothing for her to do but accept defeat and for us to go.

The rain did not stop until after we returned to the Château. The Queen retired to her rooms, and I have not seen or heard from her since. The Prince was also not to be found. I suspect he simply wished to be away from me and counted his blessings that he had more time to be on his own before seeing the witch. I asked for Henri, but no one knew where he was. I chose to have a quiet dinner alone in my room, to think and reflect on the day, but Clarissa came to see me.

She knocked on my door and I asked the attendant to allow her to enter. In her hands, she held a bouquet of fresh flowers from the side garden. She offered them to me. "Will you see me?"

I took the flowers from her and smelled them. "Of course, you are my friend." I dismissed my attendant and she curtsied and left us alone.

"We have not seen much of each other as of late and I wished to be certain." She saw my meal on the table and stood by the doorway. "Maybe it would be best if I came back after you have eaten?"

I had not seen her in such a nervous state before and my heart went out to her. "Please, sit with me and we will talk and eat."

She curtsied before me and sat the table close beside me. I saw with clear vision that our argument had caused a deeper rift between us than I had thought. I would need to take care to repair our friendship. "Would you like some cheese?"

"No, I truly want to know if you are well."

"The witch would not see us."

"How is that possible?" asked Clarissa.

"With magic, she protected her home so that the men-at-arms could not break through her door and window." I passed the bowl of fresh strawberries, knowing she loved the fruit.

Clarissa accepted and popped a ripped berry into her mouth. "The Queen then went to the door and it opened but…" I paused, on purpose, and ate a berry, taking a moment to relish the sweet flavor.

My friend swatted at my hand and laughed. I ate another strawberry and she cried out, "Cin, come now, do not toy with me so! What did the Queen see inside?"

I smiled and then continued, "She found only this note."

I handed the scroll to Clarissa. She wiped her hands and with great gentleness unrolled it. She read the words written with great care and asked, "What does it mean?"

"I do not know, but the Queen told us that the house was empty inside except for the scroll." I took a sip of wine and then leaned back, looking out the window. "She told us to return on June 17 during the full moon."

Clarissa took a strawberry and dipped it into some cream. "I would like to meet this witch." She sat back in her chair. "A woman who can defy the Queen and all of her guard has great power."

"I know." Fairy Godmother, I remembered your warning but remained quiet.

"What will you do?"

"I will do my best to avoid the Queen for the next few days."

We laughed together and spent the rest of the evening healing our damaged friendship. She had no news of Henri and I changed the topic, thinking it best that I not show my concern. Clarissa has been my closest friend for the last few years, and she knows me well. There would be plenty of time over the next week to talk more.

I do wonder, though, of the magic that the witch has and worry what might come to pass if I do not follow her instruction when we return next week. Yet today has been long, rainy, and I am tired. Bonne nuit!

June 11

I have kept quiet for the past several days, yet I can no longer keep close my thoughts. I have searched for Henri, and Joséphine informed me that he would be in Paris for some time.

I miss him. He and I have spent much time together, and I wish to see him before we see the witch. His smile and warmth are absent in my life and I miss him. I will write nothing else today as I have written enough.

Dear Cinderella,

It is with great joy that I tell you that I am on the last leg of my journey back to you. Your patience has been so great and the trials that you have gone through are nearly over. In the darkest part of night, have hope, as I am almost returned to you.

Your heart is heavy, but I would advise that you allow yourself to love. Listen to your heart, for it will never steer you wrong. When you see the witch next week, be on your guard but know where your heart lies and steel yourself to what you desire.

The path is in front of you, you only simply need to make your choice. When we are reconciled, I will protect you and make certain that you are safe. Be strong, as our time of reunion is almost at hand.

Yours,

The Faerie Godmother

June 14

Thank you, thank you for your letter. The words you have written have helped ease my heart. I also have good news to share with you, as Henri has returned! I sought him out and after dinner this evening he and I walked the gardens. I will be honest with you. I pretended to be not feeling well and went to bed early, yet then met him at the Temple of Love late at night.

When I arrived, the near full moon hung high in the sky and its light reflected off the pond. On seeing him, my heart soared and I gave him a chaste embrace. "I am happy to meet with you once again."

He returned my embrace and asked, "Are you free to be with me now?"

"None know where I am, so I am safe." From behind where he stood, a fox, appearing to have silver fur in the moonlight, crept out of the bushes and trotted off to his hunt.

Henri watched the fox go and kept quiet for a moment too long for my patience. "Joséphine has said that in a few days you return to the witch, as she refused to see the Queen."

"Yes, that is true." I took his hand in mine and asked, "Where have you been all this time? I have missed you."

"I had some personal business to attend." He turned away.

"Are you angry at me for words I said or how I have treated you?"

He looked back at me and shook his head. "No, I am not."

"Then why are you so cold toward me?" I squeezed his hand. "Why is there such winter in your heart?"

"Your worry is unfounded as I am fine." He did not let go of my hand. "The days have been long, as I have had much work to do and tonight I am tired."

"Are you certain that you are not angry with me?" I asked.

"I am not." He looked up at the moon and sighed. "Tomorrow let Clarissa, you and I have a day of fun in the garden. We will be merry, and in the daylight I will be much refreshed after some rest."

"I would like that." I let his hand go and headed back to sleep.

I am happy he has returned and that we have seen each other. My heart is full of hope for tomorrow as I, too, need sleep to help me feel refreshed. I know Henri is troubled, yet he will not speak with me, and I will respect him. However, I would be false to say that my heart did not soar to see him again.

I feel calm and at peace. I had missed him so. I will be patient, for tomorrow will be our day to enjoy. Good night!

June 15

Today, Clarissa, Henri and I took a long walk on the Château's grounds, and we enjoyed the warmer weather. Clarissa decided that she would be in charge for today. The rules were simple: No talking about the witch, the Queen or the Prince. I thought her rules fair, and we all agreed to adhere to them with the upmost care. Around mid-day we collapsed in sheer exhaustion at the Temple of Love and leaned against the pillars, looking out at the water. Henri had brought a basket with him and we sat down, eating cheese, bread and some tasty cured meats. And having great foresight, he brought two bottles of wine. Though we did not have glasses, I am not too proud to admit that we took turns drinking from the bottle.

To frolic in the sun and not worry, was much needed medicine for me. I had a wonderful day of delight. I laughed most when Henri stood next to the statue of Cupid and pretended to share a drink with him. I was relaxed and at peace without worrying about my future.

After we ate, we sat together, Clarissa and I, listening to Henri play a song on his lute. It was a rising song of joy and goodness, inspiring Clarissa to pull me up and dance. We spun around, a little too fast, and I knew her intentions. She kept pulling me away from the Temple, dancing toward the pond until she lost her footing and pulled me in. I went along with the charade and splashed her.

Laughing at us, Henri came over with his lute and sang louder until Clarissa and I exited the water and chased him until he surrendered and allowed us to pull him into the water with us. When we finished playing in the water, I chased him out of the pond and ran after him. He waited for me behind several large bushes and grabbed him. I squealed in laughter, but he pulled me close, kissed me full on the mouth and then took me in his arms. He smiled and then pushed me away and ran off.

I did not know how to respond, so caught off guard from his display of emotion was I. Clarissa found me breathing deeply, leaning against a tree and she grabbed my hand leading me back to the Temple.

The sun was warm, so we lay down in the shade of the temple and relaxed. Henri wandered back, singing a song, and after some more wine and another hour of drying off, we headed back home, content and happy.

Twilight had changed all the colors of the day to a magical world of orange, blue and pink clouds. I imagined fairies flying around, changing the palace grounds to a world of vivid imagination, and I closed my eyes and stopped. I took in a breath of air and laughed. Clarissa thought me ill and that I was delirious, yet I simply was happy and at peace. I had a wonderful day with two great friends.

I fell asleep early but awoke in the middle of the night. I went to my closet and found my glass slippers, thinking of you. Taking them in my arms, I went outside and they began to softly glow. Was this your message to me, letting me know that you were on your way to me? Their light soothed me and felt warm and tingly on my hands. The further I walked away from the Château, the brighter they became. I put them on, and they continued to glow, pulsing now, calling me away. I walked for a bit, but being outside in the middle of the night, wearing only my nightgown and glowing glass slippers, I decided to turn around and come back to my room.

I stopped to take in the beauty of the night and I crossed paths with that fox again from the other night. On seeing me, he stopped and waited, looking at me. He appeared a brilliant, beautiful silver in the moonlight, with a wide and bushy tail. A noise off in the bushes startled him and he ran off.

Before returning to my room, I glanced up at the sky into the deep darkness littered with tiny pinpoints of light. Yet up ahead by the trees surrounding the Château, I could see flashes from dozens of fireflies. I did not fully understand why my slippers had begun to glow, but my guess is that you had sent me a message of hope. I returned to my room and will now go to sleep.

We will see what tomorrow brings. Thank you for today. Thank you. Good night.

June 16

The Queen asked me to attend her today. Tomorrow we will visit the witch again, and I am in a concerned state of mind and anxious. I had not seen the Queen since we last visited the witch, and I did not know her mind as she had remained secluded and distant. When I entered her chambers, I curtsied low, waiting to be spoken to.

"Daughter, how do you fare?" She raised her arm, commanding me to rise.

I had not heard her use such an endearing term with me before. "I am well Your Majesty. I look forward to our trip tomorrow."

"Do not lie to me. I can detect falsehoods with ease, as I have lived with the King and my son for many years." She gestured to me and pointed to a chair. "Let us talk."

I kept my eyes lowered and sat in the chair trying to keep my hands still. "Yes, Your Majesty."

"Have you seen my son of late?" She adjusted her hair and called an attendant to her side to help her with her wig.

"No, I have not seen him since I last saw you." I spoke the truth and waited, wondering what she truly wanted.

After the attendant finished, the Queen clapped her hands and shouted, "Leave me."

Three women cleared the room with much haste. I did not know what she would say to me, so I remained quiet and waited.

"I wish to ask you a question, and how you answer is of the upmost importance."

I tried to remain calm but failed. "Of course, Your Majesty."

She looked into my eyes and asked, "Is Henri your lover?"

A question I have not wished to have asked of me or to share with even you, my dear Fairy Godmother! How was I to answer? The longer I waited to respond, the worse my situation would appear to be. I allowed my heart to feel as Reason knows not and said, "Yes, he is."

I lowered my eyes and waited for her to strike me. I prepared myself for her wrath and clenched my fists at my side, feeling my heart beat strong and fast within. I chanced to look at her, and she remained calm. "It is not to be unexpected, as my son has treated you with the upmost contempt. He has not heeded my wishes."

I made to speak, but she held up a finger to silence me.

79

"We leave tomorrow to see the witch and I want you both to reconcile tonight." She leaned forward and asked, "Will you speak with him when I send him to you?"

"He is my husband and I am duty bound."

The Queen laughed. "When I was young, I used to think as you. I see much of myself in you. But now I am older, I question the men around me more. You would do well to listen to the advice I will give to you."

I had become frozen with fear, as I did not know her intentions and purpose.

She took pity on me and squeezed my hand. "Although my son's dalliances with women are well known in court, you would do well to keep your secret. Tell no one, especially Clarissa. Jealousy of another woman over a man has been known to rip asunder the strongest of bonds. Heed what I say."

"Yes, Your Majesty." I nodded and kept my voice low in deference to her.

"Look at me." She snapped her fingers and startled me.

I lifted my face slightly and looked into her eyes.

"We are in my private chamber. When I call you, a Princess of the realm, you will be yourself to me. We are women and need to work through the machinations of our men."

"But, Your Majesty…."

She shook her head and said, "Just speak the words. Let them flow from your lips as they would to your friends. I do not have all evening."

"I have not seen the Prince since we returned from the witch, and our relationship is strained."

"George is not an easy man to live with, yet he will be King one day, and we need an heir. Tonight when you see my son, tell him that you will let him go and will not fight him over his mistresses." She saw my reaction and held up her hand. "Simply tell him that you will start your own affair of the heart."

"But he will become angry with me, and we will argue."

The Queen stood up, reached for a glass of wine, and took a sip first before answering. "Men often pursue their courses, thinking that they will escape from the perceived chains around their necks, but they return soon enough when they realize that they will no longer have power over you. Their reputations are precious to them."

She offered me a glass of wine and I accepted. "To take such a chance, is risky."

"Yes, but your relationship with my son has always been off center. No man will want to be known as a cuckold. He will storm off and be angry, but he will come back to you, as he knows it is my wish that you have a child together."

"You are the Prince's mother, and I am ashamed that you have learned of my indiscretions."

"I am surprised that you remained true to my son for so long a time. His blatant disregard of you has swayed me to your cause. Speak your mind to him and show him your strength. All depends on this." She drained the glass and motioned to the door. "Go prepare yourself. I will send him to you within the hour."

I stood and curtsied low. "Yes, Your Majesty."

Her eyes never left me as I backed out of the room, and when I departed her chamber I rushed back to my own to write. I have been writing with such haste that my words are somewhat unclear, and my left hand is tingling. I will finish now and write later, after I have spoken with my husband.

Late in the day on June 16

The Prince and I have met and talked. I am tired, for it is near midnight, and tomorrow morning we head back to meet with the witch. When the Prince came to my chamber, he sat on a sofa across from me and asked, "How are you, my wife?"

I looked at him and saw his clean shaven face, his strong jaw, dark, thick hair, and that boyish charm on his face. "I am not happy with you."

He ran his hand through his hair. "I am not happy, either. I tire of this game we play."

"Then it seems we are both in agreement on this." I folded my hands in my lap and said the words I had been practicing to say for the last hour. "I release you from your husbandly duties and have decided that I will no longer disapprove of your having mistresses."

His eyebrow rose and he leaned forward. "Do you jest?" Caution emanated from him.

I sighed and took a deep breath. "No. I have thought this through and, as you are a man of the world, I will accept your choices."

"Incredulous!" He smiled and leaned back, falling into my trap.

I smiled back at him and said, "Provided you understand that I will conduct an affair of my own as well."

His face turned dark and he shouted, "You will do no such thing. As my wife, you will do as I wish!"

Fairy Godmother, I do not know how I remained calm. I kept my hands tightly locked together in my lap and replied, "I, with respect, will decline your wish, as I will have a lover of my own."

I had pushed too far and he jumped up off the sofa and rushed at me. His face only inches from my own. "I am your husband and you will obey my will."

"You are my husband only in name, and as you do not respect me then we must come to an agreement." I watched his face, and he eyed me with suspicion. "You have already chosen your path and now I am informing you of mine."

"This does not sit well with me." He pulled back and sat back down on the sofa, realizing he treaded on weak ground. His knew his mother's fondness for me.

"There is no trust between us, and you can promise me that you will stop seeing your mistresses, but I see in your face that you would just lie to me." I put my left hand to my throat and felt my hand become so warm and tingle with my emotion. "I will speak to your mother and the men that follow you will report back to me. I will not be treated unjustly. Or, if I am, then you shall be treated the same."

He picked up a glass and looked to throw it across the room, but restrained himself. He remained quiet, and I had a sudden idea. I leaned forward and with gentleness I touched his arm. He pulled back away slightly. I kept my hand on his forearm and the burning question that had been on my mind for so long rose up within. Yet I feared to say the words as the truth might damage me.

"George, have you ever loved me?" I waited for his response as my world had been fortified by my belief. All my hope stayed firm on this one question.

"I do not know."

He stood and paced around the room. I moved back to my sofa and waited, as I could see him working the words through his mind, hammering the phrases into shapes that might cross the gap between us.

"When we first met, my mother pushed for our marriage. I thought it quaint how we had met. You were mysterious to me. We danced at the ball and it was exhilarating to be with you and see that everyone had eyes on us. After I found out that you were a commoner, I started to feel differently."

"But why did you marry me?"

He stopped pacing and faced me. "I felt pressured to do so. I know my mother wanted me to have a child to protect our lineage and, if I am honest, I admit that I was happy to see the people rally around us. There was magic in it and I was made part of this great story. Now I see my path, taking the place of my father and I will be fixed on a path I have no freedom to control. In these years I have left, I wish to be free to do as I please."

I was hurt and angry, but I had been with him long enough to know that he spoke his heart. He was on a boat, far away, drifting on a lake, and no words of mine would change his course. He was separate and not with me. I realized this as we spoke, and our marriage dissolved in front of me as I truly understood that he had chosen to be unmarried to me. He had already made the decision, and it was only my ignorance that kept him my husband. My threat to have an affair hurt only his manly pride and did not awaken any love he had for me.

I stood up and walked over to him. "What should we do?"

He laughed. "Mother wants us to have a child. We will go see that witch tomorrow, get the magic potion and we will have a child, raising him up as the future King."

He took a deep breath and took my hand. "It is not that I would dislike having a child with you. Rather, I only wish to explore the world and enjoy life. I do not wish to have a child now, nor do I wish to settle down in the role my mother has prepared for me."

What words could I say to him? I did truly understand the weight that he had on him. I remembered my love for him and the first time I saw him across the ballroom and smiled. I squeezed his hands and felt their warmth and said, "I understand your fear and what you desire. I truly do."

He looked me in the eyes and said, "You have always been good to me. I have treated you badly but I must be honest now. I do not love you. I have pretended long enough."

He thought a moment, scratching his several day old beard. "The choices set out before us are clear. If we want to live at the castle, we have to raise a child together, yet I do not wish that."

I could see my life with him clearly on his face. I had been a distraction, a fun companion for a time, but now he wanted to move on. I wanted so many things, but not the life he offered.

"What are you going to do?" I asked.

He did not answer at once. He pulled back and laughed. "Do? What can I do? If I go back with you, we will need to pretend that we are happy and then come to an understanding. If I choose to leave, well, I am unable to do that as my mother would chase me to the ends of the Earth. So I will stay. Tomorrow we will see the witch, return home, and have a child so that everyone can be happy."

He had not asked me what I wanted or how I felt. Wave after wave of anger and grief washed over me. I had always kept his feelings in the forefront of all my decisions because I wanted to make certain that he was cared for and loved. I had seen how his parents treated him, but his response was to rebel and back away.

My life stretched out in front of me and I envisioned being with him. We would be civil to each other. He would have his lovers and go on his adventures. In time, he would come to accept my taking a lover, and I would have a child. The witch could fix my problem for me, and the world would continue to see us as a happy couple.

Everyone would be happy—except me. I would always want more. I have a choice in front of me, and I do not remember what else we said to each other. He left my room and I stared out at the gardens, listening to the crickets. He had made his decision of half-heartedly committing himself to returning home with me. The years we had spent together had been of no importance to him. I think because he was the Prince that I had always elevated him in my thoughts, for that is what one should do for royalty. It is what is expected, proper and right. I wondered how I would go forward, and my heart ached, but it was not over losing him. Dear Fairy Godmother, my heart ached not for him but upon realizing that I had allowed myself to truly believe in the fairy tale. I am off to bed now, for I do not feel well. I need some rest to help me prepare for tomorrow.

June 17

I have had some rest and would like to write before the Queen calls me to leave to see the witch. Before I sat down to write this, I took my glass slippers out and put them on my bed. Today I will wear them, as they are my luck charm, and maybe some of their magic will help me with the witch. I must admit that I am frightened a bit. I do not know what to expect in seeing her, nor do I know what she looks like. I only know that she holds my fate in her hands, and I want our visit with her to be ended quickly. I will write as soon as I am able.

Late in the day on June 17

I have learned that I am with child.

I have so much I wish to write and put down here, for I want to be truthful. Oh, dear God, thank you for the bountiful gift you have given me!

Fairy Godmother, I will expound on all that that happened today at the witch's. Let me start at the beginning. After I last wrote in this diary, I met the Queen and Prince for breakfast, and we then left by carriage to keep our appointment with the witch. We remained quiet on the journey, as I watched out the carriage's window at the beautiful warm day that was so unlike the last time we visited. I did get to see the fields of sunflowers that the countryside is so known for in the summer. The flowers had not yet bloomed, but they were beautiful all the same. During the ride, the Prince stared out his window with a look of disinterest on his face and the Queen kept her eyes closed, seemingly relaxed, but I imagined she was praying for magic to heal the rift that had occurred between her son and me.

After some time, the Captain of the Queen's guard informed us that we had arrived, and the Queen exited the carriage first. With great interest, I looked out the carriage's window, seeing her go into the house. She was admitted without trouble this time, and several minutes later she came out and was escorted back to the carriage.

The door was opened for her and she climbed back inside—her face a mask, hard to read. I looked at her expectedly and took a breath, sat back in my seat and folded my hands. Patience would do me well today.

"The witch wishes to see you alone." The Queen nodded to the nearest guard, who still held the door, and he opened it for me.

I climbed past my husband, who ignored me and said not a word, and asked, "What should I do?"

The Queen thought for a moment and replied, "Be true."

I took the hand of the guard and he helped me down the carriage's stairs. I turned back and saw the Queen and Prince and felt this divide as though I were walking onward to another life, leaving them behind.

When I arrived at the door, it was opened for me and I went inside. A strong, earthy herbal smell saturated the house as dried plants hung from one corner of the room. There were a table and chairs on the right, and the hearth on the left. The fire burned brightly on the warm day.

Coming out from the other room in the house, the witch entered. I had not known what to expect, but she did not appear as I had imagined. Tiny, slight of build and of middle age, she wore her hair down, and her loose fitting clothes suited her well. She had no shoes on her feet, and there were markings on her left shoulder. When she came toward me, she smiled and asked me to sit down by the table. I did so and waited. I did not know what would happen. For a few moments, an uncomfortable silence drifted between us and she reached across the table to take my hands in hers. She turned my hands over, studied my palms and traced the lines there with her finger.

Then she smiled warmly at me. I remember that she offered me some tea and her voice was so melodic and free as though she had no fears or concerns. I declined the tea and asked, "What is your name?"

She poured herself some tea from a kettle on the table. "My name is Renée. What is yours?" Her English clear and nearly without an accent.

I told her my real name and she smiled, putting down the tea. "It has been a long time since you have used that, has it not?"

I remained quiet, unsure what to say, and she then took pity on me and changed the subject. "You are not here to discuss your name, but you have another question for me. What is it?"

I took a moment to focus my thoughts and concentrate on what I wanted to say. Then I asked, "Can you help me become pregnant?"

She responded right away which surprised me. "No, I cannot do that." I must have flinched in fear and disappointment because she added quickly, "Because you do not need my help. You are already pregnant."

Her words are still ringing in my head. I have longed to write those words down to prove to myself that I had not dreamed them up and that I had heard truthfully. I am pregnant now, I am with child.

After Renée told me that I was pregnant, I did not believe her and thought she joked. She asked if I felt some queasiness in the morning, tenderness in my breasts, and a veil was lifted from my eyes so that I could see clearly. I have attributed how I have been feeling to worry and stress. My days have been filled with much concern.

Renée sipped more tea and placed the cup down on the table and waited for me to calm. I had so many questions and she could see through me. "You did not know that you were pregnant?"

I nodded and started to say something but remained quiet.

"No one knows who the father is, do they?"

She had seen through me. I truly did not know that I was with child or I would have shared this great and wonderful news with you. All these years I thought that I was barren, but that is not the truth. On May 12, Henri and I took comfort in each other, and now I am with his child. I wonder what he will say once I tell him. My life is now changed, and all that I thought once set in stone has been uprooted and moved. Yet let me continue my story. Please, have patience with me and forgive my withholding such intimate details from you. I have been afraid to admit my true feelings for Henri, for I am ashamed.

For some time, I sat quiet and filled with such surprise and joy. Tears of happiness streamed down my face, and I could not stop crying. Renée hugged me, and for a good long while I rested in her arms. I said some things I do not quite remember, but she was strong, firm and helpful. When I had regained my composure, she again offered me some tea, which I now accepted.

Renée watched me sip my drink, and I could see her eyeing me up as I composed myself. I wiped the tears from my face and fiddled with the ribbons on my dress. I looked at her and asked, "What am I to do?"

She reached across the table and took my hand. "You have choices…."

I cut her off before she went any further. I was adamant about the baby.

She squeezed my hand and told me to relax. "No, that is not what I meant. I have watched you long enough. I know you want the child. What I mean is that you have choices. You can lie about who the father is, or you can tell the truth. When you leave here, however, the Queen will want to know what I have told you."

With all my strength, I wrapped all of her words around my heart. I needed to make a decision. Never had I imagined that she would tell me that I was pregnant! I know that sounds so naïve of me, but I have believed that I am barren and the possibilities in my life have been limited by that belief.

I needed time to think and I told Renée that, but she again pressed her point home and asked me again, "What do you want to do?"

She let go of my hand, stood up and came to stand behind me, covering my eyes with her hand. I could smell the Earth on her, and I relaxed, comforted by her power. "Close your eyes and be at peace."

I did as she bade me and let my mind go free.

"What do you want to do?"

Her question was simple, and I have been too worried about what the Queen would think of my decision. I realized that there was no magic in Renée's question, and no potion to fix the problem. For the first time in my life, it is with great joy that I realized that I simply needed to close my eyes, block out what others wanted me to do, and be free. You would be proud of me for the strength of character I exhibited. For a few moments, I just breathed and cleared my mind, saying the first words that passed through my mind. "I want to have this baby and live in peace."

Renée pulled her hand away and walked in front of me, sitting down on the chair beside me. "Then what do you want to do?"

I thought for a moment and realized that if I lied, I could tell the Queen that the baby was her grandchild, and then she would take me in with open arms and I would be happy in the palace. She would believe me because she wanted an heir to the throne. The Prince would know that I did not tell the truth, but perpetuating the lie would be easy for him. His mother would be happy, and he would be free to pursue other activities. I would remain a

Princess and raise my child to be a noble who would be right and true. Henri would not need to know of my decision, as my relation with my husband is a private affair. He might suspect that he was the father, but he would have no proof and, as I could easily distance myself from him, there would be no problems. I would have my happily ever after, and no one would know. In time, the lie would become the truth, for would be buried and forgotten.

Fairy Godmother, I realized at that moment as I closed my eyes that my decision would set me on a path from which I could not easily return. I listened to my heart and thought about what decision to make, and I felt a tingling in my left hand, and the moment froze in time. I imagined my future and that of my child's and how happy we would be together and how simple the path could be. After a moment or two of time to reflect, I opened my eyes and told Renée, "I do not wish to raise this baby at the palace, yet I have nowhere to live."

I could not lie, as it was not within me to do so and, in my heart, my love for Henri stayed firm. I did not wish to lose him or to live a life in which he did not know the truth and my feelings for him. Yet I had no means to sustain myself or my child.

Renée held me, comforted me, and simply said, "I will help you."

Her words soothed me and although I had only just met her, I sensed that she could be trusted. I sat with Renée for quite some time, and after I stopped crying I wiped the tears from my eyes and asked, "What am I to do now?"

Renée stood up and smiled. "Do not be afraid. I can help you, but only to a point."

I thought about the Queen and the Prince waiting for me outside. I could sense their frustration as my visit with Renée was probably taking longer than they had expected. Men-at-arms stood at the ready to whisk me away and bring me back to the Château so that I would be secure.

"I do not want to return with them." I stared at my hands, nervous. "Can you help me?"

"I can help you for some time, but there are some things that you must do on your own. Do you understand?" Renée waited.

"I will face them. I will tell them now. But will you protect me if the Queen sends the guards after me?"

Renée started to braid her hair, twisting it up. She quickly finished adjusting her hair and grinned. "No one will harm you."

I took a deep breath and smelled all the scents in Renée's home. A mix of emotion washed over me, and I did not know that my senses could be so full. "Where will I stay?" And then another thought crossed my mind, "Can you help me see Henri so that I can talk with him alone?"

Renée nodded. "For now, you can stay with me. We will discuss what you wish to do from here another time. And, as for your Henri, he might come searching for you."

I gathered myself and told Renée that I was ready. She hugged me and went to the door, opening it. I could see the guards waiting outside. They stepped back as Renée came out. The Queen stood there and the Prince sat in the carriage, half-asleep.

Step by step I came out of Renée's home, and a wave of anxiety engulfed me. I folded my hands over my belly and walked past Renée to face the Queen. I was surprised to see that she had chosen not to wait in the carriage. The sun, hot and strong, beat down on us, and the air was humid and full.

The Queen read the scene well, coming up to me and asking, "What has happened?"

How was I to answer? What words could I use to convince her that my path no longer was with her son? And would God forgive me for the vow I had broken and for the path I was about to take? The good that I had tried to achieve had turned sour and false. All that I had believed had become clouded and cold. My life with the Prince had been over and politics would not be why I stayed. I needed to make a choice for myself, and I looked up at the Queen and spoke the truth. I do not remember my exact words, but I asked to speak with her and the Prince in private.

She dismissed her guards, asking them to keep the townsfolk away. They created a perimeter and blocked traffic from Renée's home. We had a semblance of privacy. It would be enough for us to talk. The Queen rapped on the carriage door, and her son awoke with a start. He gathered himself and came to stand beside his mother.

I looked at the two of them as they came toward me. We would talk in front of Renée's home. The discussion would be private and would change all of our lives forever. When they stood before me, I curtsied to the Queen and she raised her eyebrows at me, wondering.

I felt Renée's presence beside me and focused on what I would say.

"Your Majesty, I have learned that I am pregnant, yet your son is not the father."

The Prince stumbled back as though hit by a physical blow. The look of disgust on his face said more than he ever could. "Do you speak the truth?"

I nodded at him and then curtsied low to the Queen. "Your Majesty, I wish to leave your son and have decided to relinquish my title and forfeit all my rights as his wife." I then turned to the Prince and said, "I am sorry. Whatever I could do to ease your life, I will do, but I must go."

I finished speaking and turned to go. I do not remember what she said, but the Queen reached for my arm and then swung at my face. I could see her rage and the fury there, but I was protected. Time itself seemed to slow, and Renée simply raised her finger and said, "No."

In mid-swing, the Queen's arm stopped. She was powerless. I could see her about to call for her guards, but she remembered the last time. She could not beat magic. The Prince grabbed at his mother's arm and said, "Let her go. We will finally be free of her."

The Queen struggled for a moment and then let her arm drop to her side. Leaning forward, she spat her words, low and full of rage. "We took you in, elevated you, and you rut like a dog. Is that how you repay our kindness?"

I opened my heart to her. "Your Majesty, I am sorry. Thank you for all that you have done for me. Goodbye."

I had nothing more that I could say. What words could I use, and what difference would they make? She would remain angry at me, and the Prince would do the same. Only because he had not wounded me was he upset, for he realized that his power over me had ended. He had obtained his freedom, in a sense, but I wondered how long it would take him to realize that he could not have children of his own.

The Queen, still too angry to think clearly said, "I do not command you to leave. Stay."

I stopped and curtsied low. I raised my head to make eye contact with her and replied, "Thank you for all you have done for me. Goodbye."

Renée took hold of my hand and faced the Queen. "Your Majesty, it is time for you to go. Our paths diverge here. Let her go."

She clenched her fists, and her face and neck appeared spotted with color. Her anger was fierce and strong. The Prince turned away and pulled at his mother. He saw no reason to stay. For a moment the Queen faced Renée and then backed away. She said nothing else, but the Prince continued to direct her to the carriage. He said some words to her, and his mother laughed. At the clap of her hands, her guards came back and one helped her into the carriage. In moments they were gone, and I stood beside Renée, free.

It is late at night, and as I write this I wonder what will become of the first book of my diary that is back at the Château. I spoke to Renée about my concerns, and she said that she would help me retrieve it. I do not know how, but I trust her. It has been a long day. I have had a good dinner, a bit spicy, and now I am to rest. In the morning, I will talk with Renée about my future and decide where I will go next. I am free, yet I am also frightened. And in my mind, I think of Henri. I wish to see him and tell him the news and express my love for him without fear and without reserve. I wish to be a bright star that shines forth in the night and, together, we will be steady and at peace. Such is my wish. Good night.

Dear Cinderella,

The news that you have shared fills me with great joy! I am nearly at your side and I will support and help you so that you can have your child in peace and in happiness.

Go to Henri and tell him of your love. When I arrive, I will assist you both, and your new life will begin. Delay not!

With great fondness,

Your Faerie Godmother

June 18

Dear Fairy Godmother,

Thank you for your letter. I have much to tell you! Today I woke up in a small bed filled with straw, and I looked out the window at the sun and just smiled. I smelled bread baking in the kitchen and freshly brewed coffee. I talked with Renée this morning, and she told me to relax and take my time in getting up. She also gave me a gift—the book that I wrote last night's entry in and now I am writing this one. I have eaten some bread, smeared with lots of cheese, and had some of Renée's wonderful coffee.

It is mid-day now, and I have cleaned myself up and had some privacy to myself, as Renée had gone off to run some errands. I walked around her home and I went back to sleep for a while, lying there staring out the window. As I was alone, I put my hands on my belly and the wonderful thought that I had not dreamed it, that I was truly pregnant, washed over me. The weight of my fears had lifted from me during the course of the night as I did not fear being summoned to the Queen. I realized, for the first time in years, that I could do whatever I wanted, and those thoughts settled in my mind.

I am going to sleep now and see what the rest of the day brings me. I will accept Renée's generous offer of help.

Late in the evening on June 18

Renée is sleeping, and I have time to settle my thoughts and to write. My left-hand often itches and tingles when I would like to write but have not made time to do so. I take this as a sign that my thoughts need to be inscribed on the page and shared as they will then find peace on their own.

I have been thinking of Henri. I miss him and wish to head back to the Château and to talk with him. I have feared that the Queen would tell him the news or that the Prince would murder him for his actions. My mind has been without rest, thinking of these dreadful scenarios, but Renée has used her gift of sight and has assured me that my Henri is safe.

We will go to him soon, and I have played the scene in my head until I have memorized the words. I love him, and am now not ashamed to admit my heart's feelings. His light is like the sun, and I will bask in his warmth with great happiness and contentment. Soon we will have such great joy, for we will have the freedom to be together. I am filled with such happiness. But it is late, and I must rest now.

June 23

Several days ago Renée discussed our plans for heading to the Château. I had done much thinking, and I longed to see Clarissa and to talk with Henri. I wanted to share my news with him and to tell him of my love.

Renée said that she could help me but that she needed some time to obtain the horses. We left the next day for the Château, and I must admit that I did not know how Renée would enable us to pass through the Château's gates. Yet once there, she announced us to the guards, and we were told that the Queen and her party had returned home. They had left in a rush yesterday. I realized then how little I had in the world. I had the dress on my back, my glass slippers, a borrowed pair of shoes from Renée and the book and writing instruments she had given me.

Joséphine was kind enough to have us inside for some tea, and I told her my story and she informed us that the Queen had come back, ordered her attendants to pack, and they had left yesterday around mid-day. She did not know what had happened and had worried about me. She shared with me that the Prince had asked to see Henri, but that Henri had left for the city earlier in the day. Clarissa had wanted to stay to find me, but the Queen had ordered her to return without haste. The exact details of what had transpired remained secret, but Joséphine had pieced enough together to sense that jealousy and a love affair had turned sour, forfeiting Henri's life if the Prince found him.

We now await Henri so that I can talk with him and share with him the news. Joséphine sent her best men to search for him and they expect him to return from Paris within the day, now that the Queen and the rest of the royal party have returned to England.

I thanked Joséphine for all her kindness, and when we left her chamber I had a heavy heart, as I worried about my future. I began to think that maybe my decision to stay with Renée was impulsive. I will stop writing here because I my mind is full of worry. I need your help, for much is uncertain. When will you come to help me?

Dear Cinderella,

Now, at last, we are at the crossroads where I am so near to you, yet so far. I am on the other side of a doorway that only you can help me cross through. For me to help you, you must help me break through this last barrier. I have traveled far to return to you, yet I this last wall is blocked to me.

Henri is the key to unlocking your heart. Speak your truth to him and open your heart and mind. Allow yourself to be true and honest and then your love will do the rest.

You have trusted me all these years, and I have not steered you wrong. Now, for the last few days, we are close to being reunited, yet the magic that holds me from you imprisons me. There are words that I would write to you, but cannot, as I am blocked by an enemy greater than you can imagine. I have resisted for years, and it is with all honesty and truth that a greater force lurks to destroy all you have worked so hard to build. My words may seem foreign and strange now, but I implore you to cross through this last barrier to me.

Open your mind, release it, and, once unlocked, I will be at your side. Together, we will restore all that was lost and bid adieu to the rest. Do not stray, fear not, and go to him soon!

Yours,

The Faerie Godmother

June 25

News has returned that Henri has been taken back to England. Joséphine informed me this morning. The Captain of the Guard gave her men a letter, signed with the Queen's seal. I read the words on the page with great caution, and my heart turned somber and heavy inside. Henri had chosen to be the guest of the Queen, and she requested that I return to England and her family with great speed.

The lies lay thick on the page, and the Queen's controlling hand clearly dictated the terms that I would adhere to or all would be lost. If I stayed in France to live on my own, I suspect that Henri would die in prison in England, and I would be responsible. I have the power to save him.

Renée offered to help me, and she told me of her plan. We would pack our bags and head north to Calais. From there, we would take a boat to cross the Channel to get me back to my homeland.

We left with much haste, thanking Joséphine and promising to bring Henri back to her, as she considers him family. Her offer of assistance we declined, for both Renée and I thought best to not involve any others in our plan. Confident and resolute, Renée told me to fear not and that we would return to save him.

We left the Château with a heavy heart. The events that have unfolded weigh heavy on my mind, as my worst fears have come to be. We traveled along the trade routes, stopping by each village, where Renée was greeted with much warmth. I learned that many respected her as a witch because she helped those in need.

That night, at dusk, we stopped at a large farm and Renée asked the farmer if we could stay in his barn. The older man who worked on the land was overjoyed and welcomed us both into his home. We had a warm place to sleep, tied up our horses, fed them, and gave them plenty of water. I had only the bags on my horses in which I kept my glass slippers, my journal and writing instruments.

The night was clear and brilliantly lit, the moon high in the sky. I thought I saw a fox running behind the farmer's barn, and I hoped that it would not go after the chickens. The farmer had invited his family and locals from the surrounding farms to celebrate Renée's arrival. Tables were set up outside, and delicious food was served. Our hosts shared with us an abundance of fresh fruit, vegetables and dried meats with crusty bread. We drank wine, sang, danced for hours, and I was taught folk songs. For a while, I forgot my sorrow and the problems that lay before us. The people of this tiny village truly loved Renée and were honored by her presence. I watched how she worked with them, how patient she was, being a good listener as she helped heal them. Unlike the balls I often attended at the palace, people talked to each other here, and they told stories about their day, the hardships they were up against or the funny stories that happened to them during their daily tasks.

I could see the life that these people led and that they worked hard. I saw the calluses on the men's and women's hands. There were no nobles here. The people who came to this gathering worked the land, and their lives were closer to what I had grown up in than the one I had married into. Toward the end of the night, the music turned more wistful and people went home, and I tried my best to remember the names of all the people I had met. Renée had no difficulty remembering these people, for she had a great memory, and it embraced the histories of people from years ago.

I asked her about the people later, and she told me that she remembered the stories they told her, and over the years she grew to care and love them. I still did not understand who Renée was and how she used magic, but I understood enough that she was respected and well loved. I trust that as she had helped these people over the years, so she would help me find Henri and rescue him.

After midnight, I went to the barn and slept in a fresh bit of hay. I smelled the earthiness of the barn and listened to the breathing of our horses. I just rested and took my time to think. Renée was out saying her goodnight to the surrounding families and, worried as I was, I had enjoyed the time I had that night. I had had a rough life with my stepmother and stepsisters, and then I married the Prince and fell into the insanity of life at the court. I had never truly had time to be on my own and make decisions for myself. I often regretted that. I fell directly into marriage, leaving one bad life behind and drowning in the Queen's world. She ruled back home, and I did not truly realize the extent of her power over my everyday life until recently. I had to attend to her every wish. Now I began to understand why the Prince would run off on his adventures: he simply wanted to be left alone. His actions and how he treated me were not to be excused or, at this juncture, forgiven, as he had lacked remorse. Now Henri was their prisoner, and my disbelief at the events would not dispel them. The fact remained that the Queen had captured Henri and used him as a pawn in her game. Fairy Godmother, now I understand your letter to me. A greater power does resist us and I will not bow to her. I will go to Henri and rescue him. How to do that, I cannot say.

I turned away from the light of the moon, closed my eyes, and fell asleep. I had a restless night, one filled with odd dreams. I saw myself in a foreign land, listening to the natives as they told me their problems. I listened and tried to help them the best I could. I remember being happy in the dream and coming back home to my daughter. What an odd little dream. I have wondered if I am having a boy or a girl. I do not know when I will be able to write again, as we will need to travel by boat to reach England. I wanted to write down my thoughts, for I would like to review these entries later, after I have had time to reflect on all that has happened to me. Right now, I am rushed for time and filled with many emotions.

June 26

Renée and I are back in my homeland. The trip back was uneventful, as the weather is fine this time of year. We crossed the channel without any difficulty and headed toward the castle. With limited amounts of coin, Renée suggested that we go to town, and I agreed, taking the opportunity to stop back home to see my father at his work. He was pleased to see me but filled with worry, as he had issues to deal with because of the troubles overseas. Wars, trade route disputes, and lost boats consumed him. To be kind to him, he did spend time with us and made sure that we had a good dinner. He never asked if I had a place to stay because he assumed I had come to visit him from the palace. As I tried to talk to him, we kept being interrupted by his staff who needed him to make decisions about deals, pricing, and deadlines.

His world was so separate from mine, and I felt the gulf between us. I told him that I was pregnant and he smiled and hugged me. Quiet for a moment, he looked off and said that he wished that my mother were still alive to hear the good news. We talked some more about nonsense and I hugged him, saying that I might not see him again for a long time as I would be traveling. He nodded and hugged me, seeing us off.

Even if I were to tell him that I would be leaving the castle for good and starting a new life far away in another land, I do not think he would be affected by it because his world was work, and the challenges he had at home with my stepmother. I am happy that I saw him at his work because I had had enough problems lately. I surely did not need my stepmother and stepsisters complicating my situation even more. They would taunt me and turn their jealousy into pricks of steel, constantly jabbing at me. I had grown beyond that and needed to think about my own future and not my past. The past was the past and so it is.

That night Renée and I stayed at an inn on the outskirts of town. We talked long into the night about tomorrow. I would go to the castle and ask to see the Queen. I worried that she would confront me and might even harm me but Renée seemed confident that we would be safe. I doubted that as I expect some sort of confrontation and feared that she would imprison me, forcing me to stay.

Yet if I am to escape the palace and bring Henri with me, I am not certain where I will end up or where I should go. Renée has been kind to me, but I see that our paths will separate at some point. I am pregnant and will need shelter, food and people to help me as I raise my child. I am glad to see that there are good folk out in the world. I have thought about asking Clarissa to come with me, but I do not think that would be good for her, and my request would be selfish.

As for Henri, I love him and want to see him released from imprisonment at the hands of the Queen. I pray that the Prince has not hurt him. My imagination can dream up ways in which he is being tortured at my expense, and I long to see him and feel his arms around me. I love him and will see him saved. Tomorrow will be a difficult day. I will take my rest now and sleep.

June 28

I am in my old room now at the palace. How strange it is to be here now, as my life has changed. Renée is asleep in the room next door. Much has taken place, but my heart has been wary to discuss it, as the falsehoods abound around me. Yesterday Renée and I were admitted entrance to the castle, and we were granted an audience with the Queen. Before seeing her, Renée told me that her magic would protect us from harm. I trust her, and she has kept her word.

When we entered the Queen's private chamber, she met us unadorned. She wore a plain dress and had maps strewn across a large table. She appeared preoccupied.

"Come in and sit." She snapped her fingers, and an attendant rushed to us, offering food and drink. "Have your travels been well?"

Amazed that she appeared no longer angry at me, I began to talk, but Renée stepped before me and bowed low. "Your Majesty, our journey has been safe, and your welcoming us is of great assistance."

Turning her gaze to me, the Queen asked, "How fare you, my daughter?"

I tried to conceal my surprise and curtsied low. "I am well, Your Majesty."

"Good." She put the maps down and thought for a moment. "Good. Your well-being is of great interest to us, as you would expect."

"I understand my importance to you." I remained curtsied, showing my deference to her.

She raised her hand and pointed to the nearest sofa. We followed her instruction and sat, both of us silent.

"Much is at stake in the world, and yet we squabble over the littlest of things." She picked up a map from the table and walked over to Renée, showing it to her. "What assistance could you and your sisters offer us if we wished to forge an alliance with you?

I did not understand the question and turned to Renée. She studied the map, one of Africa, and replied, "I would need to know more of your mind."

"Are you able to speak for your sisterhood in these matters?" The Queen stood before me, but I did not follow her line of questioning.

"Yes, I can." Renée leaned back and waited. Her long, brown hair was tied up nicely, and a look of curiosity crossed her face.

"Good. We are in need of your assistance, and I am willing to negotiate terms." She appeared to glide away from us and poured herself a glass of wine. An attendant rushed to pour her a drink, and she dismissed her from the room with a wave of her hand. "More is at stake than the future heir to the throne. Tell me, what do you know of Napoleon and of his campaign in Egypt?"

"Pauline, one of our sisterhood, has taken to be his mistress there. She calls herself Cleopatra and has been distracting him from the wars."

"Good, good." The Queen walked to the table littered with maps and picked up several loose sheets of paper. She waved them in the air and said, "We intercepted several of his letters to Joséphine and will have them published in the London papers. In a few weeks, much of England and France will know of his private feelings about her betrayal of their love, as she has also taken a lover."

I stayed quiet, unsure of what words to speak.

"The news you share will be of great help to my sisters and me." Renée leaned forward and said, "What is your plan?"

"It is simple. Napoleon must fall. He intends to conquer all of Europe and then England, and that must not come to pass."

"We are in agreement."

The Queen turned to me and asked, "Where do you fit in to this large puzzle, my dear?"

I could not speak, as I did not know the answer.

Renée offered one for me and replied, "I am to meet with the sisters soon."

"The convocation starts next week, does it not?" The Queen waited to read Renée's response.

"Yes, that is true." Renée tried to conceal her surprise. "I plan on leaving to attend directly from here."

The Queen nodded. "Cinderella, what do you know of war?"

I was not prepared for the question and answered from the heart. "Not much, Your Majesty. I am innocent in those affairs."

"And you, what know you of war?" The Queen sat down on a plain chair and rested her head in her hand.

"I know of what you ask." Renée looked at me and then back at the Queen. "You refer to the spirit of War."

The Queen smiled. "Exactly."

"Your knowledge of the ways of the Fey is impressive."

The Queen took pity on me and said, "You wonder what we speak of?"

"Your Majesty, I am aware of my shortcomings and understand my place. I ask no questions now as I do not know which questions to ask without appearing to be a fool."

The Queen laughed. "You are wise for your age."

Renée stood up and reached out her hands, concentrating with her eyes closed. The Queen walked over to us and remained silent. I could hear Renée mumble some words in a language that I did not understand, and both the Queen and I waited.

After a few moments, Renée opened her eyes and faced the Queen. "It is not near. We are safe for now."

I looked around the room in fear. "What is not near?"

"The spirit of War." The Queen pointed to the map in her hand and showed me all of Europe. Marked were listings of where English forces fought against Napoleon's armies. "Beneath the world we see, in the shadow, there still holds sway the Lord of the Fey."

Renée held up her hand in warning. "Do not speak his name."

The Queen nodded and observed Renée's caution as she glanced around the room, searching for some unseen thing. "War, pestilence and famine are spirits that faeries can control and spread through the souls of men."

I listened and began searching the room myself as the Queen went on. "The tendrils of War bleed across Europe and search for a foothold here. I and others fight to prevent that from happening."

Renée took my hand and said, "Your mother also fought against the spirit of War."

"You knew my mother?" Dozens of questions rose up within.

Renée nodded. "Yes, I did, and I will tell you more later. It is not safe here for long."

"She is right and our time here must be concluded soon." The Queen hurried on and faced Renée. "We need your help to remain strong. Will you go to your sisters and advocate for us?"

"She must come with me." Renée took my hand and held it firm. "And we must see that Henri has not been harmed, nor will be. He must have his freedom."

The Queen asked me, "Do you agree to these terms?"

"Yes, I do."

"Then I propose that you both go to the convocation and bring our message of assistance to the sisterhood. Henri will remain here, secure from harm, to meet you both when you return."

Renée glanced at me, and for several moments I hesitated, wanting to stay with Henri, but the Queen had compromised and promised him no harm. Now it would do me well to consent, so I nodded. "We agree."

"We have our understanding then. Go see your Henri and talk with him. Tomorrow let your journey begin."

The Queen dismissed us, and with quickness we left her private chamber. I now had more questions than answers, yet I made straight for Henri. Though I feared for his safety, I learned that my concerns were unfounded, as he had a room of his own and was not in chains. Renée begged fatigue and went to her room. The Queen's assistant led me to my love.

When I entered his room, he lay on the floor, reading a book. He did not see me, and I watched him silently. The attendant left me, and I held back for a moment, looking at him, wondering what I would say and the words that I would speak. I had much to tell him, and my mind could not comprehend his response.

After some time, he sensed me, turned around, and a look of confusion crossed his face. Then he smiled and tossed the book aside to come and embrace me with much warmth. I embraced him, and he kissed me.

"Are you in good spirits and are being treated well?" I held him close.

"Yes, the Queen has been good to me, and I am of good spirits." He looked at me and asked, "Why have you come home? I was told that you had chosen to travel through my country with the witch to learn her ways."

Fairy Godmother, my strength left me. He did not know that I was with child. The Queen had remained quiet. All of my fears of him being harmed were not true. I stared into his eyes and I wanted him to love and choose to be with me. Yet my understanding with the Queen held firm in my mind, and as I had only known that I was with child for such a short amount of time I had not the courage to tell him my state and that he was the father of our child. I was a coward and feared his rejecting me.

Instead I said, "I have come to collect some personal items for my trip with Renée." I released him and told him part of the truth. "I will return in several weeks and hope you will wait for me."

He smiled. "I am enjoying myself here as I learn of your English ways." He picked up the book he had been reading and placed it on a table. "Your Queen has been kind to me, and Clarissa has helped to show me your ways. She is a good friend."

"Clarissa has been my constant companion the years I have lived here, and I trust her beyond words." I folded my hands over my belly and had thoughts to tell him that I was pregnant, but again I remained silent.

"Yes, she is of good comfort and I enjoy her company."

He turned from me, and a thought rushed through to me. "Are you my friend?"

"Bien sûr!" He laughed and the sound of his voice calmed me.

"When I return, I long to spend time with you."

"We will walk the gardens here, talk of poetry, and be as before." He bounded off and pulled a book from a shelf. "I have already begun a new epic poem that I will share with you."

"Where is your lute?" I saw no sight of it in his chamber.

"In your country, I am learning that poetry is more respected and I have chosen to study and write."

He showed me his book, and his charm was infectious. Our conversation was pleasant and light. Neither the Queen nor the Prince had informed him of my state, and I had time yet to talk with Renée and ask her for her advice. I turned my mind toward the convocation of witches and my impending journey. Renée had her reasons, but I suspect she wanted me close with her on the journey, for then we would plan my future. The doors to my happiness would remain open, for I suspected that the Queen and Prince would accept my child as of royal blood if I maintained my silence. My husband would do as he wished with the women of his choice, and Henri could be my lover here at the castle. We would raise an heir to the throne, and all would be stable and of comfort.

The Queen's compromise and understanding did leave me more at ease with the concerns that had weighed heavy on my mind. Tomorrow Renée and I would leave this castle, and I would have time to reflect on my future and that of my child's. My lack of will to tell Henri the truth weighs on me. I continue to be afraid that I will lose him if I tell him my condition. I must rest now as it is late and we leave early tomorrow. I pray to see you soon.

Dear Cinderella,

I am here now, and we are close to being reunited. The wall that separates us is thin and I have seen you in your room, writing and crying from your hurt. If I could embrace you and take away your suffering, I would because what you write in your diary is tamer than what you experience and feel. I see that you are strong and filled with a desire to help others. The path you are to tread is one of which you must be certain. I cannot tell you more, as the enemy blocks me from you. The energy that surrounds you is restraining me from helping you. I cannot break through on my own, and I ask only this of you: Release your mind of rational thought and allow your heart to rule.

Be careful on your journey, and I will remain patient, waiting for the time that I can see you. My magic cannot cross the frontier before me but I will help you as soon as I can. My gifts to you now are my words of comfort. The hurt you feel, I can feel. I know you long for him to come to you, to show you he loves you, and I admire your choice to remain quiet about your child.

We cannot see the future. But if Henri does not stand by you and your child, then I will. I will not desert you. I will be with you through to the end. You must trust me. Allow yourself to feel. Your emotions will unlock the door between us.

Yours,

The Faerie Godmother

JULY 1

Dear Fairy Godmother,

Thank you for your letter. With each word I write, I will listen more to my heart. I do believe we will be together soon. Today Renée and I began the journey to the convocation of witches. When we left the castle, Clarissa came to see us and I hugged her, and we shed tears. She wished me a safe journey, and I longed to talk with her to tell her my secret, but I did not. I asked her to be Henri's friend while away and said that I would return soon enough. Once returned, there would be plenty of time for me to share with her my news. I would need her help with the baby and hoped she would be happy for me.

Renée and I drove our horses away from the castle and soon we were on our own. We talked for some time, and I told her that I would like to visit my mother's grave before we left my homeland.

After my mother died, my father spent a large sum of money to honor her memory by having her buried in a beautiful mausoleum. It is of modest size and I have not visited it often, but I did wish to pray there and wish my mother's spirit well. When we arrived at the cemetery, I told Renée that I wanted to be alone.

I walked through the gates and had some trouble remembering which direction to head, so I asked a groundskeeper the way. Today was warm, sunny, and there were few clouds in the sky. I ran my fingers over the engraving of my mother's name and the dates of her birth and death on the door to the mausoleum, wondering if she could aid me now. I often wonder what she would have thought of my marrying the Prince and if she would have been able to resist the Queen's ploys.

I have had a difficult life, but I know my circumstances are not dire compared to others who have no food or shelter. To even complain about my condition would be laughable to so many because I married into the royal family. Yet the hurt and loss I still feel from my mother's passing is a dull ache inside, and I wonder if I can ever come to peace with her death. I will always miss her, and the emptiness I feel is a secret oasis of solitude. I can retreat into myself and look around me, seeing the world and all of its possibilities. But I can never reclaim what is lost, and those conversations that would have so helped me now will never take place. Her guidance in my choice to marry the Prince and even my loving Henri cannot ever be discussed. When I came to visit her today, I simply wanted to say goodbye. I hope to return soon to see Clarissa again. As for Henri, my heart is full, and I worry about us. I miss him and yet I know that my path is with Renée because the bargain I made with the Queen must be filled.

I kissed my mother's name on the mausoleum, said a quiet prayer, and then turned to go. But before I left, I saw a fox, silver in the daylight, run in front of the mausoleum's doors, seemingly protecting the gravesite. I waited a moment and the fox stared at me, unafraid, and I let it all go. I need to leave my mother behind. The fox could not harm her as she was already gone. I left the cemetery, and I found Renée shortly after.

She came close to me and asked, "Are you okay?"

I tried to hid my feelings from her, but could not. I felt too ill at ease. "Tell me how you knew my mother."

Renée thought a moment and sighed. "I knew your mother when we were young. We learned magic together."

"Were you childhood friends?"

"No. I did not meet your mother until I was near 17 years of age. We studied at the same school together and became fast friends."

I wanted to walk away from the cemetery, for my heart was heavy. Renée followed me and we walked our horses away from the gates. "What was she like back then?"

"Full of smiles and mischief, to be honest. Your mother pulled me into much trouble." Renée laughed and added, "But we had so much fun together."

"And now she is dead and I still miss her more than I could ever have imagined."

Renée put her arm around me and simply said, "Soon you will be a mother."

I nodded, and we lapsed into silence, walking toward the nearest farm. After such a day, we decided to stay the night in the farmer's barn, as crossing the Channel would be safest tomorrow. Once we settled in, Renée went to talk with the farmer because one of his cows has been sick. I am sitting at a desk, writing at the end of the day. The twilight colors of deep blue are fading into black, and the oil lamp beside me is casting a yellow and orange glow.

I am thinking of my child growing within, and yet know that my belly will not begin to show for months yet. Soon I will be a mother. For now, I need time to think and to simply be. I have exhausted myself today and for my own well-being I need to go rest. I will stare at the sky, looking for the moon and hoping that one day I will be more settled. I cannot see any further ahead on my path than what this oil lamp bestows on me. And I must accept that.

July 11

Our journey has been good, and I have not made much time to write, as we have traveled much in the last week. Renée and I head to the southeastern part of France, and on our way we have stopped in many a village to meet with the people, help those in need, and I have learned much of Renée and of her abilities. She has often made potions for the sick or for those in need.

The days on the road are long, but we have taken a leisurely pace, staying each night at a different town or village. After several years of living under the Queen's watchful eye, I feel at peace. We stay in whatever home will take us in and, at first, I was worried that we would not have a place to rest our heads at night. On only one night did we not have a place, and we tied up our horses, found them water by a creek, and fell asleep under the stars. In the middle of the night, I awoke to pass some water and I glanced over at Renée. She was at peace, sleeping deeply, and did not hear me get up and walk away. On the way back to the blanket, I glanced up at the sky and was amazed. The beauty I beheld was breathtaking. I continued to walk back and decided to veer off and head toward the water. I was not far from where we camped. The sound of the running water drew me closer and I walked to the banks, climbed down, and put my feet into the cool water. I closed my eyes and listened. I could hear the crickets and felt the mud between my toes. The earthy presence of being washed over me and I opened up and began to cry. It was not at a particular situation or memory, but I wanted to release all of my sorrow and hurt.

After a few moments I wiped my eyes, and a feeling came over me. My ability to describe the feeling is lacking. I can best say that I felt alive and a part of Nature. I could feel the world around me, and I put my arms up and imagined light coming from my hands and that energy seeped into the world around me, making me stronger as I gave of myself to Nature. I sensed the animals near me, and all the insects and creatures I could not name became part of me and I of them. I could see, hear, and smell life strong and vibrant. My life had begun, and the life within me continued to grow. I glanced down and thought I saw a light in the water, but it was only the reflection of the moon.

I walked out of the water and back to the blanket. Renée had turned on her side and I closed my eyes, listening to the world. I fell asleep in minutes, but it was the first time that I had listened to Nature's lullaby. I had been too much in the world, and I had allowed myself to forget Nature and the beauty around me. Jewels, balls, shoes and clothes—these intoxicants I had breathed in, thinking that they would save me, but they were only entrapments. I am seeing how my life was and wonder what my life will be. I am more at peace now, and as I observe what Renée does and how she moves through the world, I am most impressed.

For me, I am starting to see the path in front of me. When I was younger, I thought my stepmother would rule my world. She did as long as I allowed her to. When the Prince married me and I moved away with him, I fell into another prison, and I lived in the palace. I had thought that my world would forever be dominated by the Queen. Now I begin to know a different path I can take and a new life I can live. I do not fully understand what my role will be, but I take comfort that I am not meant to. Today, the today as I write this, is warm, inviting, and full of sun. I will give myself more time and will not write here often, as I want to live in the world. I want to embrace the time I have now to learn what I am meant to do and where I am to go. My life, the life of my child, is before me, and I want to make a good choice for us.

July 14

Today we celebrated the anniversary of the revolution with a small village. We danced, laughed, and had a delicious meal for our supper. I never thought that I would be celebrating the overthrow of a King, but the people here are happy without monarchs. I wonder if the royal family in England ever worry about their subjects being infected by the desire to revolt. I would suspect that the Queen has had concerns about such anarchy, and she has taken steps to prevent revolution from spreading to England's shores.

I did enjoy myself today, though, and after all the celebrating and dancing Renée sat down with me and wanted to talk. I have been waiting for this discussion to take place for days now, but I was glad that she gave me time to think.

Renée sat down on a pile of hay, and we listened to the music and laughter coming from the front of the barn. Many of the surrounding farmers still danced and made merry. She had a piece of straw in her mouth and she asked, "Are you feeling well?"

"I feel not as nauseous today as I have on this journey." Loud bangs on a drum distracted me for a moment, and then I continued. "I am more comfortable today."

"We will be at Reims in two days and there the rest of the sisterhood will gather. At the Roman arches in the city, we will meet and begin the convocation."

"Do you think the sisterhood will help against Napoleon?"

Renée stood up, ignoring my question and danced to the music that wafted through the air. She pulled me up, and I danced along with her, and she started to laugh. When the song ended, she took a few minutes to breathe and then said, "Worry will only bring you more worry. The sisterhood is already fighting Napoleon. I do not go on this journey for the Queen, but for you."

I sat back down on the fresh pile of hay and wiped sweat from my brow. "But why?"

"You ask yourself that question." Renée smiled and flopped herself back down on the hay. "Pourquoi?"

"Will you not tell me what I need to know?"

Renée laughed at me and shook her head in defiance. I know she had had much wine, and I had doubts as to her clarity of thought.

113

"You will learn soon enough, as the sun follows the moon." She threw some hay at me and then ran off to join the merry makers, celebrating the victory over the dead King.

I sat there, tired and with child as I approached near two months. Renée has been kind to me, and I know she means me well. In the time that I have known her, we have not talked much about her past or of her powers. I have not seen her use magic often. And there is no fire and brimstone in her powers—at least none that I have ever seen. Dear Fairy Godmother, I remember seeing your magic as you changed a pumpkin to a carriage and mice into horses. The light that emanated from your magic wand was beautiful to behold, but I have not seen any of that type of magic from Renée. And what of your warning about her months ago? I am still wary of her at times.

I tire and begin to ramble. Let me go to sleep thinking of today's enjoyment, be thankful for my friend and for the child growing with me. Good night!

July 17

Maybe I have made a mistake. I do not know. It is late, probably the middle of the night, and I woke from a nightmare. I cannot remember the full dream but I remember looking at myself in a mirror and seeing that most of my hair had fallen out. Several sores covered the bald spots, and I touched them in the dream, feeling the dried encrusted blood. In the dream, Henri had left me, and I was alone and sick. I woke up scared and frightened. I have these doubts that I cannot dispel. Yet I must try.

Tonight we are staying at a merchant's house on the outskirts of Reims. Tomorrow Renée and I are to meet the rest of the witches from the surrounding area, and I am worried again.

I worry most about my child. What will become of her if something happens to me? I do not have close kin near me, and the family I do have are not able to really nurture a child the way I would like. After I woke from the nightmare, I went outside and looked up at the sky. The darkness was complete, and a cool breeze comforted me somewhat. I kept walking, drawn to what, I do not know, but I could not stop. I needed to walk, and I turned back and saw the dark shape of the house. No other houses were nearby and as we were in the outskirts of the city, a field of sunflowers filled the fields behind the house. I walked next to the flowers and, being barefoot, watched my step, being sure not to step in a way that I might stumble and hurt myself.

The moon hung low in the sky, giving just enough light to help me walk along the dirt path. A slight breeze blew, rattling a hanging chime off in the back of the house. I heard nothing else except my own breathing and footfalls as I continued to walk. After several minutes, I stopped and sat down on the cool grass. I stared back at the house and then up at the sky and wondered if what I was doing was right. Was this the best course of action for me? Should I have stayed with Henri and been at the mercy of the Queen? I missed him with all my heart. There was no way to tell if my current path would prove best.

I stood and continued walking and, having turned around, saw a fox in my path. He was large, and with the low moon he appeared to have a silver coat of fur. I have often seen foxes on my walks at night, curious as to what the creature would do. He sniffed at me and then ran toward the barn, disappearing from view. Fully awake from my slumber, I headed back to bed as I had woken with a purpose but, when I had thought that I had remembered, the feeling left me again, and I felt like a fool walking in the dark. The nightmare hung over me still, but I came back to bed to write by lantern light. My left hand is beginning to itch from my writing too long, and I will take that as a sign that I must to bed. Tomorrow is a big day. I will meet the other witches, and I wonder if I will feel as ill at ease as I do now. Maybe it is best that I stop writing and get some sleep. Tomorrow will be a long day.

July 18

The first day of the witches gathering is finally over. It is almost midnight, and I want to do some writing so that I will not forget all that I learned today. When Renée and I arrived, I expected there to be hundreds, if not thousands of witches. Instead, we met several dozen women of various ages. A circle was formed on the grass by the Roman arch, and we all sat down. For the first hour, witches announced themselves and told from where they had come. I quickly lost track of their names and whether they were coming from the South or the East. In the late morning, a fire was started and we came together to make food for us all. I must admit that I found listening to some of the witches to be challenging, as I simply wanted to fall asleep.

Toward the end of the first day we again came together to have dinner. We cooked together and shared stories. Once we had our full, we sat in a large circle, and two of the elders told stories of their lives. I learned much about the witches. The day was filled with each telling their stories and sharing information about the lands they lived in. Most shared information about herb lore, the political situation in the country, relationships with surrounding areas, and their dealings with the Church.

Tomorrow the witches will talk about plans for the upcoming year and placements for the sisterhood throughout France and parts of Europe. Renée has shared with me that how the sisterhood can help thwart Napoleon will also be discussed.

Midnight has passed as I write this, so I should be sleeping but I need to write. I have neglected dealing with the thoughts on my mind for quite some time as the journey has helped to distract me from how I am feeling. Yet tonight I choose to address how I feel. What I write, I write for myself. After we had dinner this evening, the gathering of witches ended for the day, and we met with some of the families from Reims. There was singing, dancing, and more food. I attracted the eye of a young man. He is the son of a blacksmith, well-built, handsome, and strong. He danced with me, and I saw many of the witches pairing off with men of their own. He asked me to join him in a local barn but I declined. He tried with smiles, his charm and humor to win me, but I had to refuse him. My heart is tied to Henri and my thoughts are ever thinking of him. When I close my eyes, I can see his face, hear his laugh, and feel the touch of his hand on mine.

I left the young blacksmith and headed off on my own, away from the dancing and celebration. I regret now not having spoken to Henri and not telling him about my pregnancy. I admit that I feared his reaction. I imagined that if I were to tell him the truth that he might leave me and go to a distant sea, and I would be left without support and his love. I miss him and daily I wonder why I am on this journey. I want to go to him and for us to hold each other. I have his child growing inside of me and I am here, in a strange city, with women I have never met before.

I long to build a love with Henri that stretches across time into the here and now. Damned be all the challenges and fears that are inside me! I am tired of choices that will be easiest for me rather than what I want. I am weak, so weak, but I want to be with him even though I am afraid that he will not wish to be with me. Or worse, I fear that he is a free spirit who wanders the world, loving as he will. My hunger for his soul would devour him whole, extinguishing the light I love so much and in that goodness would turn dark as all that I loved in him would die. My will would crush his spirit, and he would despise me as I tried to hold him down. I fear this. In the center of my being, I am afraid of this desire that has built itself within my heart.

When I close my eyes, I see him still. I see us standing in the gardens of the Château near the Temple of Love. Clarissa is playing in the water, and I will soon follow. The day is warm, our bodies fresh and strong, and his smile is like the sun. I am drinking in his memory and my eyes can see, reliving his touch and the feel of his hands on my face as he looked into my eyes and we saw into each other. Our spirits are so close that they touch against time, distance and distraction. I remember how we snuck a kiss when Clarissa could not see and the taste of him lingered on my lips and we smiled at each other forever. Time stopped, my heart called to him and we put away our doubts and for that moment, that single, solitary moment, we were one.

I knew him, he allowed me to see him as he truly was so young and bright and sure of himself. He began to sing and the laughter in his song was healing and true. I gave myself to him, in my mind, I said, "Yes." Yes to the joy of it all, yes to our mutual need and desire and yes to all that I am and would be and to his limitations and faults. I spoke to Love and opened my soul to him. In that day, that moment our hearts and minds fused together for that fleeting moment and we were happy and one yet separate and ourselves. My heart is so full, and I miss him so much. I want to be with him now, but I am so far away. I am his in my heart and mind. I will always be his and he will be for me. Will he choose me and stay with me when I return? Dear God, please help me with this hurt that I feel. It is so heavy on my soul.

Oh, God. My hand itches and burns with the brightness of the sun! This feeling of warmth floods through me, embraces me, and with all of my soul I call to him. I cast my thoughts to him and say his name in my heart. Henri. Henri. Henri, I am yours. I see us now. Oh, God, what is happening? What do I see on this page? What is… My God…

Cinderella's Secret Diary (Book 1: Lost)

Dear Cinderella,

I have come. Your heart has unlocked the door that I could not come through. I am here now and will see you tomorrow. Look for me as I will be there.

Love,

The Faerie Godmother

July 19

I need to try to put down into words what I have done. What I can do. I have taken time to go through the day and I left the book after what happened. I was afraid and unsure of what I had done. When I first started to write my diary passages, I prayed that they would help me find my Fairy Godmother and that through my words I could reach her again and she could help save me. Now she has come to me today, and I will share with you all that has happened. But first I want you to know that with these words, I now write to you, my daughter, to explain to you my power. My mother could not teach me what I needed to know, but I shall share with you what I have learned, for one day you will need this knowledge.

I have stumbled upon a wonderful part of me that is beginning to unfold and blossom. I do not know when you will read these words, but my diary will be my gift to you. And I am unfettered now, willing to become someone new.

When I last wrote, I had closed my eyes and I imagined Henri and I being together. The sun, the laughter, and how happy we were. My writing hand (my left) began to feel warm, and I opened my eyes to see that my hand glowed brilliantly like the light from the full moon. Startled, I opened my hand and, by accident, touched the page. There, as you can see above, the picture of the Temple of Love appeared. The image rose out of the page and then settled back, colors blending and mixing, alive with power, and the soft scent of vanilla washed over me. Transfixed, I stared in awe at the page and watched the image take its final shape and then settle. Hours later, the image remains.

As it was after midnight, I tried to go to sleep, but Renée heard me and came to speak with me. She sat next to me on my bed and smiled. I did not know why. "Has it happened?"

"Has what happened?" I kept looking down at my left hand in fear that it was on fire.

"Have you experienced the first taste of your power?"

I did not answer at first. I opened and closed my hand a few times and then nodded.

Renée took my hand and squeezed it. "I have been waiting for this day for more than nine years. I cannot tell you how happy I am."

Questions filled my mind, and I did not know what to say. I wanted sleep, but I also wanted answers. "Do you know what has happened to me?"

"Yes, I do." She grabbed my hands in hers and squeezed them tight. "Let us not wake up the farmer and his family. I will tell you what you want to know."

Possibly because I was worried and had just stumbled upon my magic powers, I turned away from her. "If you have known for years that I had such powers, why did you not come to find me and speak to me before this?"

Her face softened as tears were in her eyes and her voice was choked with emotion. "Every witch must discover her powers on her own. It was not for me to show or tell you. I would have done you more harm than good."

"And how have you known about this for near a decade? Have you spied on me from afar? Who are you?" I pulled away from her in concern.

"Yes, from time to time, I have looked in on you from afar." She sat back against the wall and sighed. "I knew that without your mother the truth would never be easy for you to learn."

"But how did you know of me?"

"Your mother and I were close friends for years after we left school. We were close until she left for England, though we agreed to write letters and remain in touch."

I sensed she told me a half-truth, but I stayed quiet. I focused on other concerns. "Yet after my mother died, I needed help, for I suffered with my stepsisters and stepmother. Why did you not intercede? I would have left them and come with you."

Renée listened to me and then waited for a moment. "I lost contact with your mother and only used my scrying magic to see you on your birthday. For right or wrong, I decided to not interfere with your life. I waited to see if fate would bring you to me."

I went to answer but she interrupted me.

"Do you think that by my coming to you and telling you that you have magic powers that you would be able to unlock them? They were yours to discover, and your life is for you to lead. Now you know your true mettle. When we first met and I told you that you were pregnant, you decided to take the harder path. You chose not to lie, to leave all that you found comfortable and safe. Your choice made you who you are now so that I can tell you what you need to know."

I did not know what to say. Angry as I was, she spoke in truth.

"We do not have much time, and I have much to tell you." She put out her hands and asked, "In time, I hope you will forgive me."

I decided to curb my anger and took her hand. Renée squeezed it gently and continued to hold on firmly. She scratched the side of her neck and swatted a fly away. "Your mother was a powerful witch with fey blood. There is darkness in the world, and your mother tried to defeat those forces but lost her battle with them. It is tradition that a witch tell her daughter of her powers at the time of her daughter's first menses. That did not happen with you, as your mother passed and then your father took care of you."

I had many questions to ask her but the most important I could not hold back. "How did you truly know my mother?"

"We were close friends for many years. After we lost touch, I did not learn of her death until months after she had passed. It was then that I tried to find a way to help you, but I learned that another had already given you assistance."

I rose up out of bed and asked, "You know my Fairy Godmother?"

"I know of this faerie that you speak." Renée took a deep breath and continued, "You must guard yourself against that faerie's magic."

"Guard myself against?" I laughed. "My Fairy Godmother helped me when I needed her most." I thought to say more, but held my tongue.

Renée watched me and then said, "You would do well to trust me and stay away from that faerie. Your mother would think it best."

"My mother?" I felt anger surge through my veins. "I have struggled alone for years and now in the middle of the night you give me advice to stay away from the only person who has been consistently kind to me?"

"You are right. I am so sorry." She looked me in the eye and backed away from me. "I thought it best not to meddle in your affairs. But now we do not have much choice as the war has spread across Europe and you have discovered your powers." She stayed quiet for a few moments and then continued, "If you would have me, I would be your mentor, teaching you the power of the sisterhood."

"What would you have me do?"

Renée replied, "You must come away with me and together we will discover your powers."

"Come away?" I stood up and walked away from her to the far side of the room. "We are on a quest for the Queen, and I have left my love to complete this task."

"Yes, I am asking you to leave all you know and come with me." She stopped herself and started again. "I did not mean to tell you all this in the middle of the night. We should stop so that you can rest and we can talk in the morning. There is no urgency to decide now."

Anger flooded through me and yet I kept quiet. I would not share with her what I knew about my Fairy Godmother or how I expected to see her in the morning. I chose to remain silent. "Yes, let me think before I decide. Yet I must know before I sleep, what is this power that I have?"

"I will not tell you. You will show me."

She put her hands at her side and relaxed her face. I could see she looked tired and vulnerable. "Take your left hand and touch my forehead."

I gently brushed my finger against her forehead, closed my eyes, and I could see myself walking at night, holding my glass slippers. I was back at the castle, still with the Prince, and it was a cool, fall night. I hurried through the woods, trying to find a way to the fairy lands, praying that I could find a way to escape and be saved from all the problems around me.

At the edge of the trail that led out of town, I walked down the road and slipped through the brush, clutching my slippers tightly. I stopped at a small puddle and on seeing the moon reflected in it, searched for some sign of fairy activity, but I saw none. I did see a fox, but he left me alone. Standing up, I held the slippers above my head and cried out for help. I focused my thoughts, coiled them within and then released all that I had been feeling.

Fear at what I might discover, hurt at the loneliness of my life, and regret for the path I had taken. Alone, unsure of myself, and so young I looked up at the slippers and they began to glow. The faint light within them gave me hope. I held the slippers close to my chest and I begged to be taken away. Someone needed to save me, to take me under her wing, and to rescue me. But the lights faded in the slippers, and my hope seeped away, fading back into the dark of night.

I opened my eyes and was back. My whole left arm glowed in a pure, white light. The light did not burn, but it lit up the room. Renée had closed her eyes, and I saw her truly. She had wrinkles around the corners of her eyes and freckles on her nose. She trusted me, and I wondered about that, unsure what other secrets she had not told me.

Her eyes opened, and she drew back slightly, taking in a breath. The light in my hand faded, and I lowered my arm.

"It was so cold that night, and you were so lonely and afraid." Renée pretended she held something in her hands and said, "I could feel the smoothness of the slippers and the warmth of their light."

"You saw everything?" I asked.

"Yes, I could see and feel all that you allowed me to."

Again, I had so many questions, but what I most wanted to know came to mind. "That memory was the first of many in which the glass slippers glowed for me. What magic is within them?"

"Your Faerie Godmother made those slippers for you, and I suspect that they are her link to you. What other powers they have, I know not. Again, I would caution you."

I ignored her warning and said, "I have many questions, but it is late." I yawned and pulled back my hair, tying it up for the night.

"Get some rest. We can talk more tomorrow." Renée hugged me and simply said, "I am happy for you. A witch discovering her powers is of great joy for the sisterhood."

I hugged her back and then climbed into bed, exhausted and filled with many questions.

July 22

I have not written for several days, and I have neglected to do so as I feared that Renée would read what I had written. I have since left her, and, as she promised, my Fairy Godmother came to visit me the morning after I discovered my powers.

I woke up late in the morning and realized that Renée had let me sleep, leaving for the convocation herself. The farmer and his family were out working the fields and I awoke to the smell of fresh bread and smoking meats. I gathered a small breakfast of honey, bread, and milk and then went outside to see the field of sunflowers. There, walking like a brilliant ray of sun, came forth my Fairy Godmother. She walked right out of the sunflowers, glowing in pure orange light, with a smile on her face.

I ran to her, and she embraced me, welcoming me in her arms. "As promised, I have come to you."

I could not believe that after more than four years she had finally returned. I went to speak but she held up her hand, quieting me.

"You have many questions, I know. And I would, too, if I were you, but we have no time. I fear that I must ask you to make a quick decision, and I will understand if you decline."

I pulled out of our embrace, trying not to wrinkle the beautiful dress she wore. "What would you have me do?"

"Your friend the witch has put protective spells around this house that keeps me from entering. She and her sisters wish to harness your abilities, for you are a powerful Chronicler, and they have need of such power. If we are to stay together, you must come with me tonight."

I knew not of what powers she spoke, but inside I knew that I had waited for years to see her again, and my feelings were clear. Yet I did have some concerns.

"I know this decision is heavy on you, but I will tell you. If you come with me tonight, we return to England to your love. You will be able to be with Henri. And you and I will work on learning how to best use your magic."

My smile broke forth on my face, and I hugged her again tightly. "Yes, I will come with you."

She kissed me on the forehead, and we made plans to meet near midnight. I went back inside, but watched my Fairy Godmother vanish back into the sunflowers. How happy I was after all this time! I came back inside and finished eating. In time, Renée returned from the convocation.

When you are older and I can share with you how to know when your powers will present themselves, I wonder what you will think of my decision to return to my homeland with the Fairy Godmother. Renée had asked me to stay with her and to leave behind all I have known to pursue the magic that runs within me, yet I longed for Henri. I needed to go back to him and tell him the truth about you.

When Renée returned to see how I fared, we had an enjoyable lunch of fresh fruit and vegetables. Then she asked me, "Have you decided what you will do?"

I had thought of withholding the truth and leaving in the night, but Renée had helped me, and I wished to be at least partly honest with her. "I do not wish to stay with you. I will head back to see the Queen and tell Henri of my love for him."

Renée put her bowl down on the table and asked, "You are firmly decided on your choice?"

"Yes, I do not wish to leave the father of my child."

"Will you forego all that you have learned for the sake of a man's love?" Renée waited a moment and then continued before I could respond. "We can teach you and help you."

"I thank you for your offer, but I have decided." I declined to meet her gaze and reached for some more fruit in silence.

"How will you return home?"

"I will be fine."

"But you are pregnant and have had problems with nausea for the last few weeks—who will be your guide?" Renée sat next to me and offered me her hand. "I will go back with you."

"No, I will make other plans."

Renée pulled her hand away from me and asked, "Why this sudden coldness to me? What have I done to offend you?"

I bit my tongue as I did not wish to confront her.

Yet Renée understood my thoughts well enough. "I suspect that you are angry at me for asking you to leave your beloved Henri." She saw my face at the mention of his name and said, "If I walked your path, I would...."

She turned away and stopped talking.

I stood up and faced her. "What would you do if you were me and you discovered that all you thought true was a lie, and that your friend simply had her own intentions in mind?"

"I would watch your tongue, as I do not lie." I could see fury in her eyes. "If you lack the wisdom, I cannot make you walk down the path. You must decide for yourself what is right. I am only concerned for your health and that of your baby."

"Truly? Or are you and your sisters interested in harnessing my powers to help you in your own plans?"

"What nonsense prevails in your mind today?" Renée slapped her hand on the wooden table. "Have I ever expressed any interest in your powers?"

"Tomorrow I will be on my own path, and you will not have to worry about me any longer either way." The early warnings that my Fairy Godmother had given to me about Renée had been true. I had not seen any of these concerns at first light, but now I understood.

"I would be well to rid myself of you for how insolent you are." She put her hands to her forehead and then said with careful deliberateness, "Your mother means too much to me to abandon you in your time of need. I will not be shaken lightly from aiding you."

"Why have you not told me that I am a Chronicler?" I accused, standing strong before her.

"How did you learn of this?" Renée stood up and stared at me in disbelief.

"What else do you know about my powers that you and your sisters hid from me?"

"We are hiding naught from you. If you stay with me, we will teach you of your powers. Do you truly know what a Chronicler is?"

"I know enough."

"Yes, enough to be dangerous to yourself and others." Renée put her hands out to me and implored. "Please, let us stop arguing and let me help you. I will answer the questions you want. Please!"

I sat on a chair in our borrowed room and asked, "Then tell me why you do not wish for me to return to Henri."

Renée bit her tongue and remained quiet.

"Tell me the truth or I leave tonight." I threatened, but my decision had already been made, and I was leaving in the evening anyway. She remained quiet, and I pointed at her, saying, "All my life I have been a pawn on the chess board, but no longer. Speak your truth to me!"

Renée dropped her arms to her side and with great anger said, "He does not truly love you, and your heart will be broken when you return to him. You long to have someone love you, and you impulsively attached yourself to him as soon as he showed interest. Do you not see this?"

"I see that you are jealous and that you wish you had a man who loved you as I have Henri."

She laughed at me, and my anger soared. Renée took a deep breath to stop laughing and then laughed some more.

I pointed at her and could feel my heart warm with power. "You have always been jealous of me! Admit it!"

Renée stopped laughing. She stood strong and replied, "Yes, I am jealous of you. I am jealous that your mother chose to leave me to return to England. I am jealous that she took your father as her husband so that she could have a means to live on her own after she left me. And, yes, I am jealous that she bore you, and that she had asked me out of her life."

I took in all her words. "What do you know of my mother?"

"Know? I know that I loved her and love her still and that even though she threw away our love, I still honor her by trying to be your protector." She spat on the floor and put her hands on her hips. "You are ungrateful and have had such luxury that you do not know the meaning of hardship. What the sisterhood and I offer you is beyond what you can know and yet you rebuke our offer of assistance? Why?"

I came close to telling her about my Fairy Godmother, but I knew that she would turn those words against me. Instead I needed to find a way to remain distant so I said, "I am in love and am pregnant. I will go back to Henri and choose not to have a part in this war and intrigue." I gathered my few belongings and threw them into my sack. In the evening, I would leave.

Renée was quiet, watching me, and then said, "Know this about being a Chronicler: You are a living historian, able not only to see events and use words to record those events, but also to allow others to experience the past. You have begun to learn that much, but your powers as a Chronicler can also reshape events."

She had attracted my attention. "What do you mean?"

Renée chose her words carefully. "With guidance and practice, you will be able to change the past."

As I listened to her words questions exploded in my consciousness, yet I remained firm. "Thank you. I need my rest now, and in the morning I will leave."

Renée started to speak, clenched her fists at her side, and then left the room. I tried to rest but had difficulty doing so. I wondered how I could learn such a skill as changing history. I had much to learn and many questions, but my choice had been set and now I would head home to see Henri. I yearned for his warmth and to speak with him again. I longed to see his smile and to talk with him about poetry, art and music. My decision made, I am headed home.

July 29

Forgive me for not writing sooner, but as you will not be able to read this until you are old enough, there truly was no urgency in my writing with quickness, yet much has happened. I have put off writing for as long as I can and, if I am honest with myself, I would prefer not to write at all. I did not have a mother to help me with the problems that I have now. I am older and one would think that I would have had more patience and wisdom, but I am a fool. As long as my magic remains in the world, only you will be able to read certain parts of this entry. I have learned how to lock my words down onto the page, not only protecting the book from natural harm, but from unwanted eyes. I have learned much in the weeks since I last wrote.

Let me start where it hurts most. My Fairy Godmother and I left France together, and I, in my naivety, trusted without question. I learned much during our journey together, as she was a patient, kind, and thoughtful teacher, showing me how to use the fey magic that runs through our veins, but now I pay the price for my foolishness. I get ahead of myself. Let me share with you the story.

When she and I arrived at the castle, my Fairy Godmother used her magic to disguise both of us. We appeared to be common townsfolk looking for work in the kitchens. I knew why she had wanted to enter the castle without announcing ourselves. She did not wish to bring us unwanted attention, and this way I would not have to face the Queen.

Once inside the castle, I searched for Clarissa to share with her my decision to tell Henri of my love and to run off with him, as I would need an ally in the castle. I searched and could not find her. When I looked in her rooms, she was not there, yet I did find a lute that lay on a table. I recognized the carvings on it and saw scrolls of music scattered throughout the room, Clarissa's room. A cold, dark fear seeped into me.

I turned to my Fairy Godmother and asked, "What should I do?"

She kept her voice low for fear of discovery and replied, "You have reason to be concerned. Go find them. I will use my magic to keep others from this part of the castle."

With purpose, I ran toward the room where I last saw Henri. Mounting worry crept over me and as if in a dream, I walked as quickly as I could. Fear crept up inside me, and darkness formed solid and furious around my heart.

I gathered myself together, and a tickling feeling came into my left hand. I then ran to Henri's room and prayed that my fears would be unfounded and that I had misunderstood, but the seeds of doubt had been planted. I had lived many years of my life in this castle. I had sacrificed so much, and my love for Henri burned righteous within me. I was in the right. His child grew within me. I was in love, and I would not be cast aside.

Several people scurried out of my way as I rushed by, and I burst into his room. What I saw is burned in my memory. Henri sat with Clarissa's head in his lap, his back against the wall, holding some sheets of paper. His words danced from his tongue as he sung to her of his love.

I rushed further into the room, and my disguise faded. He saw me, and his smile turned dark. Clarissa sat up, and a look of fear descended over her. They had been caught in their lie. Neither had ever seen me angry, and for how many years had I allowed myself to be good? I swallowed every bit of lies and nonsense handed to me, and I ignored myself. But at that moment, I decided that I would no more. I needed release and, looking back now, I am ashamed at what I did, but my anger burned bright.

Henri made to stand and talk with me, but I would have none of it. Clarissa pushed herself off of him and then stood, imploring me. "Please, I am sorry. Let us talk. I can explain."

Her words flowed out like a bird who squawked at me, and I ignored her and pushed past her.

"Calm! Calm! I can explain." In his nervousness, Henri's French accent labored forth as he came toward me with open arms.

I ignored him and brushed his hands away, resting my palm on his face. The tingling of my magic came alive and his words came to me. I could see his thoughts, how he had courted Clarissa with the same words he had me, using even some of the same songs. Unfolding before me, I could see that he had used me, and I had allowed it. His words of love were simply to fill him up with light and joy until he moved on to the next person. He had never truly opened himself to me. I had already been forgotten, and his new conquest was full in his grasp.

When the Prince and I were together, I remember the pain I had felt at learning that there were other women besides me. It hurt to look in the mirror and to keep my faith in myself, but at that point my marriage with the Prince had dissolved. I had known that we were no longer together. With Henri, my bright and beautiful Henri, I had given all of myself to him, and in return, I was a deck of cards to be tossed aside. A new toy had come and I, pregnant and alone, was of his past.

This flash of insight and memory washed over me. I heard yelling from behind me and realized that several attendants had called for assistance. Clarissa pushed herself off the floor and rushed to insert herself between Henri and me. "Please, listen!"

I pushed her away with my right arm and ignored her crying. Instead, a dark thought took seed within me. I unleashed my magic and could feel the heat in my left hand. Henri's memories opened to me and I saw the truth.

By a fountain, out in the gardens outside of the Château, he restrung his lute, and two of the French nobility asked him about me. "Are you falling in love with that English woman?"

"No, of course not!" The contempt in his voice, echoed in my head. "She is my summer diversion. A small appetizer, if you will." The nobles laughed, and the scene faded.

All the secret talks we had, the shared moments, connections between us, were an act, and his true feelings rolled off his tongue with ease. I heard him clearly. I saw the truth. He had used me to ease his boredom, and now I was no longer necessary.

I focused and stirred the dark seed within, and reservoirs of energy came to me. Black tendrils in the ether came to my beck and call and I threaded them through my hand. The light dimmed in the room, and I heard Clarissa gasp. My hand absorbed the light as I funneled my hatred and vengeance into Henri. He pulled back, but I remained calm and in his mind, I said, "Speak."

"What are you doing to me?"

"What are you doing to me?" I repeated.

He fell back against the wall, trying to flee. "Stop your dark magic on me!"

"Stop your dark magic on me!" I chanted back at him.

He pulled with all his might against me, but he could not remove my hand from his face.

"Help me get her off of me. Help me!"

I dug deeper into his thoughts and shouted, "Help me get her off of me. Help me!"

Clarissa pulled at me and screamed in fear, pleading at me to release Henri. Instead I opened myself up, and all my hatred, fear, anger, loneliness, and hurt poured out of me. His eyes unfocused and he wobbled on his feet. "I do not know what she is doing to me. But I cannot, I cannot. Stop!"

I allowed a slow smile to show and said, "I do not know what she is doing to me. But I cannot, I cannot. Stop!"

I released him, and the black tendrils in the room surged into him, blocking out the remaining light, and I left my voice in his mind. My mark, as I had cursed him.

He grabbed at the sides of his head and screamed in terror as my thoughts chased after his. Every thought he had, he would hear me repeat back to him. His betrayal of me was complete, and my revenge just and full. Clarissa, terror in her eyes, backed away from me, and at that moment I could have released my magic upon her, too, and taken them both down into the dark pit within me. The surety that I would not be powerless again and I would make them both suffer fortified me.

The light returned to the room, but the dark tendrils thickened, dropping from the sky like tar. The substance spread out, looking for victims and I pulled back, watching Henri fall to the ground, sobbing in tears.

Clarissa fell to Henri's side, shaking him and then turned to me, begging, "Release him. Please, you are hurting him!"

I stood firm. "You both deserve to suffer for what you have done."

Clarissa had no response. She looked at me as though she had never met me before, having never seen me so distraught and angry.

"I am with his child. And I returned to tell him." I knew nothing else I could say. "None of that matters now."

Realization dawned on Clarissa's face, yet she stood by Henri's side. "Please, have mercy on him."

"How do you feel right now?" My Fairy Godmother had entered the room unknown to us.

Surprised by her sudden entrance, I said the truth. "I feel free." I stared at my left hand as it pulsed with power.

"Good, allow yourself to feel this anger. Make it your own. Harden it around your heart and use it as a weapon to strike down those who would hurt you."

Clarissa looked past me and pulled Henri to her and backed away to the wall. "What is that monster?"

I turned and saw the Fairy Godmother's beautiful face, not a day older from when she had first given me my glass slippers that I now wore. "She is no monster. She is my Fairy Godmother."

Clarissa continued to pull Henri away and shield him with her own body. "Please, leave us alone."

Without a sound, my Fairy Godmother had moved next to me and whispered into my ear. "When they made love, do you think they thought of you?"

I clenched my fist and my anger surged.

She spoke softly within inches of my ear. "When he spent himself in her and she writhed in pleasure, were you in their thoughts?"

A dark rage built up within me, and I wanted to erase them both from my site. I wanted to see them suffer for their betrayal. I can admit that now. I hold now the deep shame of how much I hated them at that moment.

"Use your magic to wash them clean." My Fairy Godmother's hands were on my shoulder, and she kept whispering to me. "Release your magic, and I promise you that you will feel justice."

I raised my hand and gave in. I pulled light and air into me and my emotions swirled within, filling me.

The door breaking behind us distracted me, and I turned back, surprised to see the Prince and Renée. The Prince had his sword drawn, and he rushed toward my Fairy Godmother, yelling, "Sophia, you are deceived!"

Renée threw off her cloak and raised her hands and waved them at my Fairy Godmother.

Backing away, my Fairy Godmother released me, and my vision cleared. My anger drained from me as I watched her face shimmer, splitting into a myriad of living tendrils that peeled away, revealing the face of a fox. Half animal and human, the creature laughed, and the sound pierced through us, shivering me to my core.

With a wild lunge, the Prince tried to decapitate the creature, but the blade melted away in the air, and he fell forward, off his balance.

New arms grabbed me, and I saw Renée's face. She had cloaked herself in white magic. The black tar-like tendrils of dark energy that continued to fall from the ceiling edged back, and in my daze she shouted at me. "Release Henri, and the fox will go!"

Still drunk with power, I did not listen to her request.

Renée touched her left hand on my forehead, and I heard a chime inside. "Clear."

For a moment, I listened. I saw your father on the ground writhing in confused agony, his sanity slipping from him. Clarissa knelt by his side, comforting him, and my Fairy Godmother, now a grotesque monster that licked its chops, coming toward me. The fox creature called after me. "I will find you and visit you soon. Be fearful, for I will come for you."

It pointed at me, and my glass slippers tightened around my feet and began to pulse with an eerie yellowish light. Ignoring them for the moment, I chose to act, and with sudden clarity I realized what I had done to Henri. With a wave of my hand, I freed him. Renée pulled me close and she shifted, changing. My vision left me, and I remember flying through the window and being free. The fox creature reached for us as we shifted and flew out the window, but its reach would not suffice. We heard its guttural cry and its hatred call after us, and then it vanished from sight.

I could see the Prince going to help Clarissa and Henri, and then all faded into blackness. For a long time I fell into sleep, and Renée carried me through the clouds.

August 5

When I awoke, I lay in a bed in a room that I did not recognize. Renée was at my side. She had started a small fire in the room's fireplace, and I could smell soup in a bowl beside the bed.

"How are you feeling?" She asked.

"Tired." She offered me a drink and I accepted a small sip of water. "Where are we?" I strained to sit up but my head ached.

"We are at The Queen's House." Renée put a cool, damp cloth on my forehead, and I lay back down into the pillow. "The Prince is here, and he wishes to see you."

"I need some time before I can talk with him." I waited a moment and then continued, "Renée, I am so sorry for what I have done." I turned away from her and held back tears.

Renée took a deep breath. "What you did today was wrong, but I need for you to understand why."

My head hurt and I rubbed it. "I do not need a lecture right now. I know that I should not have cursed him."

"You will get no lecture from me. Do you know who your Faerie Godmother is, and what those dark tendrils were?"

I remained silent.

She stood, and I noticed that around the bed, in a perfect shape, she had drawn a circle of salt. "Your Faerie Godmother is the Lord of the Fey, called the Silver Fox." She pointed outside at the sky, gray and dark with rain. "Your use of dark magic brought the faerie to you, along with the spirit of War's attention, down upon everyone you ever loved."

All my memories of my mother's last night came back to me, yet I remained quiet of those feelings. I remembered her stories to me about the Silver Fox and wondered what this all meant. "I do not understand." I sat up and reached for the cup of water.

"Of course, you do not understand. You are new to your powers, and you acted on impulse and hatred. All that your mother fought to achieve has been reversed. You have called War's attention to this part of the world again and, I fear, the Lord of the Fey is fixed on you."

"I am sorry. I truly am. Is it true that I have not harmed any of them permanently?" I had never seen Renée so angry before. "Is there not a way for me to make this right?"

"There is nothing to be done. War's tendrils are seeping through the countryside, finding similar hatred and fear. And look at your feet…"

I pulled the covers off of me and could see that I wore my glass slippers. With a sickly, yellowish glow they pulsed dimly. I slipped my finger into the back of the shoe and tried to pry them off but they would not be moved.

Renée shook her head. "I tried to remove them while you slept but could not." She rested her hands on my ankle and sighed. "My magic cannot undo this bond that he has with you."

"He?" I surrendered, for the moment, still trying to remove the shoes, and asked, "Who do you mean?"

Renée lowered her voice so that I had to lean closer to hear her. "He, she, or it. The faeries are ever-changing. The Silver Fox has branded you with his mark through these shoes. It will find you wherever you go."

"But I do not understand. Why would this faerie disguise itself as my Fairy Godmother?"

"I know not its plan, as faeries are fickle yet often patient. I fear you play some great part in its grand play, and I believe your faerie Godmother has always been the Silver Fox." She stopped talking abruptly and took a pinch of salt out of a pouch she wore on her waist and threw the salt at the window. She murmured some words in a foreign tongue, and then waited, listening.

I knew not how to respond. "Are you certain of this?"

Renée turned to me and held my gaze. "No, I am not. Yet this creature does have a purpose for you, and I fear we will learn what that is with great swiftness."

I leaned over and grabbed the brush on the night table.

"Wait!" Renée tried to stop me but with great strength I smashed the brush against one of the glass slippers. The brush slid off the glass and bruised my ankle.

Renée took the brush from my hands, and I sobbed in fear and pain. "The faerie's spell cannot be broken with physical force. We will need to discover another way."

My emotions welled up within, and I continued to cry. Renée held me, and after a time I said, "I am truly sorry for leaving you. You spoke the truth and were right."

"It is not about being right, but we must work together." She wiped the tears from my eyes and pulled back to see my face. "Do you agree?"

"Yes." I nodded and held her close as I feared what I had done. "I need your help. Please forgive me my arrogance and stupidity."

Renée brushed the hair from my face and smiled. "Yes, all will be well. I loved your mother, and I will protect and help you." She covered me again with several blankets, and I lay back down to sleep. "Rest now, for in the morning we must go. The spirit of War feeds on dark magic, and your magic is too raw now. We will not be safe here for much longer."

A great fatigue washed over me, and I fell back to sleep. I will write you more later. I am spent, and filled only with regret and fear. I saw a part of me that I am ashamed of. You are my daughter and, one day, you will have power of your own.

I allowed myself to let my heart rule me. Instead of saving myself and creating my own path, I fell for Henri and lost myself in him. His brightness, so like the glorious sun, filled me with joy, and his energy lit up my life. I bathed in that light and tricked myself into believing that he truly loved me, but he did not. Yet my heart still yearns for him. I am broken inside and lost. Even knowing all of this and how he betrayed me, I still miss him.

Now I have the Lord of the Fairies fixed on me and I fear for our safety. Know this: Your mother is not perfect. I am full of anger and fear and wanting. Out of my decisions I am now pregnant with you and you must hear me. You must believe me. I would never take that back. You will grow to be your own woman, and I cannot show you the way on your path. I do not yet even know where my own path lies, but I can share with you this secret. It is not something I can tell you. It is to be shown. I will right all this wrong. I will fix what I have broken and am contrite for what I have done. I made a mistake and my anger and fear ruled me.

When you are in trouble and need to find your way, stop. Truly stop and listen to yourself. Allow yourself the freedom to be, and an answer will come to you. Watch what I will do. I will fix my mistakes. I swear it.

August 6

I awoke and saw that the Prince slept in a chair beside my bed. It was the middle of the night, and an odd, half-remembered dream of the faerie king frightened me to wakefulness, and I opened my eyes, watching the flickering of the fire as the light fell on the Prince's face. Outside a steady rain fell. I did not remember the last time I had looked at my husband and seen him asleep and vulnerable like a newborn.

I needed to shift in the bed as I felt uncomfortable, and the creaking of the bed startled him. He opened his eyes with a start and leaned forward with his hand on his sword. Still half-asleep, he tried focusing his eyes and asked, "Are you safe?"

He quickly glanced around the room, searching for trouble and, finding none, settled back into his chair and yawned.

"I am fine." I sat up, listening to a few birds that had begun to chirp outside. Though we would not see it because of the clouds, the sun would be rising in another hour. I turned to the Prince and watched as he rubbed his eyes. "Thank you for coming to rescue me."

"You are still my wife, and you always stood by me, even though I mistreated you. Though we have been estranged, and I have wronged you in the past, I will always protect you from harm."

"I appreciate your kindness." I was thankful that my belly did not show, and I thought it best to remain quiet about Henri. "Were you injured by the faerie?"

"No, it vanished as you and Renée left." He paused for a moment, choosing his words carefully and said, "We will have to decide what our future will be when this crisis has passed."

"I know." I did not wish to discuss logic and reason. Now was not the time. "We will have time enough."

He leaned over and fixed my blanket, ensuring that I was warm and shielded from the dampness in the air. "I fear there will be not time, for my mother and father have other plans for me. Rest and in the morning we will discuss more of how to protect you from harm."

"We will divorce and you will find another to maintain your family's line. I understand."

The Prince left his hand on my arm. "Go back to sleep and I will watch over you."

I squeezed his hand and smiled and then allowed sleep to draw me back into dreams.

August 7

It is decided: The Prince will take Renée and me, with an escort of guards, back to the King and Queen. A messenger has come, informing us that it is safe to return. I fear that my fate will be decided soon, and I do not know what will come from the audience with their royal majesties. I had fleeting thoughts of running away to France, but Renée convinced me to adhere to the request. We will need allies against the Lord of the Fey. I must go as I am called.

August 9

We have returned from the castle, and I have much to write but very little time. I am sleepy, but I must take this chance to write. I may not have another opportunity to write, for I fear that the Faerie Lord will come for me, but I must have you know that I did talk to your father again. And something else, my daughter, something momentous: Renée and I are going to America. America. We are to depart almost immediately. Please be patient. I will write more.

October 9

When we reached land, I was helped out of the vessel, and for a long time my legs felt unsteady. The ground swayed, for the movement of the boat stayed with me. As I write this, I am in a small cabin and safe. Fifty-eight days is a long time, and I would rather forget the long journey across the ocean. Closed quarters, lack of privacy, and much danger were our companions on our journey to the New World. I have been so thankful for Renée and her company, for my diaries were inaccessible to me, packed away as they were in my trunk, with all that I own, so little, now. Without Renée's assistance, I do not believe I could have made the crossing.

For you, time has not passed, as you will read these entries right after each other, whereas for me, nearly two months are gone, and my world has changed, unutterably. Now that I have time, let me use my skills as a Chronicler, and tell you all that has taken place.

* * *

The King frowned at us. He sat on his throne and shook his head. "The Queen trusted you to take her message to the sisterhood and instead you return to nearly destroy my kingdom."

Renée curtsied low. "Your Majesty, I take full responsibility for not properly training my charge." She glanced over at me, and I knew to remain silent.

"It is rumored that Napoleon is returning to France, and war is ripe in Europe. Now you have brought the Lord of the Fey down upon our kingdom." He focused his gaze on us and banged his hand on the arm of his throne. "We should lock you away in the tower for your misdeeds!"

The Queen's gaze shifted toward Renée and me. "Your majesty, if I may…"

She smiled at the King, and he visibly calmed. "Let us hear what you have to say."

"With the Lord of the Fey attached to our daughter-in-law, would it not be in our best interest to send her away?" The Queen spoke with disinterest, and I could see the game she played. In my heart, I thanked her.

"Yes, let us send her to France and be rid of her!" The King settled back on his throne and released his breath. He had retained control, and I suspect he partly feared what magic Renée and I could conjure forth.

Cinderella's Secret Diary (Book 1: Lost)

"I would suggest we send her to a far-away land in order to prevent Napoleon from stumbling upon these witches and harnessing their power to harm our people."

The King thought for a moment and said, "America."

"With certainty, your suggestion is most wise." The Queen turned to us and held our eyes. "Far enough from England and Europe to allow us to focus on Napoleon."

"An excellent suggestion," the King boomed.

I could see Renée unclench her fists, as the Queen's idea would suit us well. We would not be imprisoned, but and instead be given a chance to start anew in America. I understood that the Silver Fox would haunt me no matter where I went, but a new start in America was most welcome to my heart. I could barely contain my hopes for a new freedom..

"Two days from now, you will be on a trade ship headed to America." The Queen touched the King's arm lightly and he added, "As you were once part of our family, we will provide you with coin to help support you. Leave us!"

Renée and I curtsied low, and I made eye contact with the Queen and thanked her with a nod. Though I had failed her by not bearing an heir, she had not entirely abandoned me. Upon leaving the room, I wondered if I would ever see her again.

August 10

After the official ceremony dissolving my marriage, Renée and I met to talk. She asked me how I felt, and I told her that I was tired and drained. I needed rest but first needed to talk with her about the future. We talked for a good while, and I learned more about how the witches had positioned themselves in places to learn about world events and, when necessary, they helped to shift power in a different direction. Such a time had come now.

We talked yet could not agree. I wanted to go to America, but Renée wanted to escape the King and head back to France to fight against Napoleon. She clearly saw that the First Consul would rise to power, and his continuing reach would engulf many countries, putting all at risk.

But Napoleon did not concern me. I feared when the Silver Fox would return, as I knew he would. I just did not know when.

When we talked, Renée laughed sarcastically and covered her mouth with her hand. "It is all the same."

"I do not understand." I wanted to better understand her, but her reasons for helping to fight were unclear to me.

"You are so much like your mother that I am amazed."

I sat back and drank more tea, waiting for her to continue.

"Your mother and I had a disagreement before you were born. She wanted to leave my homeland and go across the Channel, marry and raise a family."

She avoided eye contact with me and I watched the lines around her eyes. I waited and just absorbed what she was truly trying to tell me.

"We argued for weeks and our time turned stale." She looked up and opened up to me. "I loved her and wanted our life to remain the same. We lived in such peace, but she saw trouble ahead. And she was unsettled. She wanted a family. I could not give her that."

She had said some of these words before, but her frankness surprised me. I had many questions I wanted to ask. I sat still and wondered aloud, "What did my mother do?"

"Your mother packed her things and left the home we had built. I refused to see her off because of how angry I was at her. She chose to sacrifice all we had."

I took Renée's hand and asked, "Why did she really go?"

"I learned later that she had used her magic and saw the spirit of War descending across all of Europe. She saw an opportunity to stop its spirit from taking hold."

I listened to her, and memories started flooding back to me. All those years ago, all that had happened, and I could see the connections now. The stories of the Silver Fox that my mother used to tell me and her bringing me into the forest time and time again had meaning now. With clarity, I began to understand my mother's motives.

Renée laughed. "And now, many years later my position is similar to hers. I want to stop War and you want to go live a quiet and peaceful life."

"I do not want to run and hide. I want to take the Faerie Lord away from those I love."

October 9

I did not think that Renée would come with me, but I suspect that she feels honor bound to do so. I am my mother's daughter, and she wishes to protect me. And, honestly, without her help I do not know how I could have survived the voyage across the sea. I felt sick for days, and she cared for me, forcing me to eat, and helped me with special tea to keep my strength up. Two storms nearly wrecked the ship, but we survived. I watched in awe of Renée's power as she shielded the boat from harm. She had an uncanny ability to protect people and those around her—extremely useful when lightning and towering waves tried to sink the ship.

We are here now in America. I will write more when I have more strength. I want to just capture this moment. It is my first day in America. When I left the boat and came on shore, I could smell such intoxicating things. There is more Earth here. No, that will not make sense to you. Let me try and explain with better clarity. I feel closer to the ground here and more centered. I can feel the energy in the dirt as it is still untested, new and open.

We did not dock in a harbor, as there are complications with ships from His Majesty landing in America. We were dropped off, given supplies, and several men came with us. The ships have already left us, traveling onward to their destination. We are now alone with several men. One, whose name is John, has made the trip back to the continent several times and knows the terrain.

Upon landing, John brought all of us to a small encampment. Tonight I will be able to sleep in the comforts of a nice bed. Renée has already started cooking and she has asked me to rest. Often I do not listen to her request because I like to help despite being tired. The nightmares I have while sleeping have increased in their intensity. The Silver Fox reaches out to me in my dreams, yet I resist him. For how long I will be able to hold him off, I do not know. Instead I try to focus on you. How wonderful for me to be able to look down and see my belly showing. You are growing inside of me, and we made the trip together.

There is a smell, a pungent herbal smell, all around me. I asked Renée about it and she wondered if we are closer to the land of the Fey here. Soon we will find out. For now, I need to rest. I cannot go on. I need to sleep.

October 10

I will share with you a little of what happened to us back in England for I have some time. Before we left, I had wanted to see Clarissa and Henri. The Queen allowed both meetings to take place with minimal protection from guards. Her continued support I cherished.

An attendant announced my arrival to Clarissa, and I walked into her room, watching her as she studied a beautiful gown laid out on a table. A seamstress worked on the sleeves and, at first, Clarissa did not see me enter.

"Come in." She found it difficult to look at me and asked, "Why have you come?"

In my heart, I wanted to blame her for her betrayal. "I wished to say goodbye before I left."

She stopped and dismissed the seamstress and her attendants. When the room had cleared, she came to me and said, "You hurt him most deeply."

"I hurt him?" I could feel my anger swell inside and focused to take a deep breath. Renée had taught me how to control my magic when anger came to me. "How could you betray me when you knew I loved him?"

"You had left him and he showed me favor." She crossed her arms and her neck turned red.

"Yet I am having his child. Do you not understand?" I implored with my arms, hoping she would see.

"But I love him!" Tears wet her cheeks.

"As did I." I knew that our friendship had dissolved, and a man had been the cause. There would be nothing to resolve our differences. "I wanted to say goodbye. I hope that in the future we might once again be friends."

Clarissa took my hand. "Goodbye and I wish you well."

I turned and had to leave, as emotions washed over me. I kept walking and heard her call to me.

When I turned back around, Clarissa threw her arms around me, hugging me tight. "I am sorry and beg for your forgiveness, yet I do love him."

I held her, and we cried together. I knew not what else to say, for my heart was broken. The love of a man had come between us.

"I am sorry for cursing Henri, yet I still love him, too." I pulled away from her and ran out of her chamber because I could say no more.

I would write more, but my heart is still so full. My friendship with Clarissa is damaged and lost. Maybe it is best that I focus on my time here in this new land.

October 12

Last night I took a walk by myself, and my fears have been realized. It was after midnight and, though probably not the safest of decisions I have made, I wanted to explore the land at night.

During my walk, I went out beyond the small encampment. From the little that I can see, it appears that the men here are trappers and that they bring back the pelts of various animals in the surrounding woods. Renée and I have begun planning where to go on our journey. With winter only a few months away and you to be born mid-winter, I will need a place to stay and raise you. I wish to continue going West, but I cannot see that far ahead. Instead, let me focus on what I did tonight.

On my walk, I could hear insects buzzing incessantly. At one point, I heard a noise behind me, and I quickly turned to see Renée standing in her dark robe behind me. She had made the noise on purpose to let me know she was there. But tonight, I did not want any company. On my walk, I simply wanted to explore and to get away. I waved Renée back and she hesitated and then backed off, leaving me alone.

I know she only wanted to protect me. The area that we are in is very remote, and it is possible that there are wild animals around. I suspect there could be bears. I went to the beach, and I took my boots off to feel the gritty sand on my feet. The shores back home had lots of pebbles and not the fine grains of sand. As I walked closer to the ocean, I could hear its soft waves tumble and crash on the beach. The water looked calm, and with a bright moon overhead I could see far. I planted my feet on the ground and opened my mind.

I was in America, on a new shore, in the sand with the glory of the ocean before me, and the old ache in my heart for Henri had begun to fade. If I listen and am still, I can hear the call of my heart. With my eyes closed, I pulled down the walls inside as Renée had taught me, opened up and let my mind flow. The beauty of it all, the smell of the ocean, and the light of the moon lit me up and I turned around, hearing his call, coming from back off the shore into the woods.

I walked away from the encampment, and the two torches from the lookout tower faded into the distance. I was entering into unclaimed land, and the trees were sparse at first, but after a few minutes I was engulfed in brush and thick trees. In the daylight, I had not seen the trees so densely populated. From the watchtower, I had seen a good stretch of marsh in this direction, but I must have been wrong. The smells changed and the salty taste in the air faded, replaced with a fragrant rush of ferns and pine. I stopped, fearing that I might trip in the dark or hurt myself, when suddenly I saw him.

He darted past me, and I jumped back, startled. A large fox ran into the foliage on my right. I saw him only for a second, but his fur looked silver in the moonlight. He looked a blur to me, and I stopped, my heart pounding. I wanted to back away and run. I was scared. The hair on my arms stood up, and my left hand tingled. I could feel power here. Yet I could not run forever.

Over the last few months Renée had trained me to notice the changes in the world around me. The static before the thunderstorm, the wind before daybreak, and the smell of fear before peril. My senses were overwhelmed with majesty and delight. I could sense a change occurring around me. With purpose, I took one step forward, and night turned to day. The change took place instantly.

It was dark, then the full sun beat down on me. I raised my hand, blocking out most of the garish light of day and understood. No longer did I stand on the shore in America. I had shifted and moved or the world had fallen beneath me, replaced with an odd mixture of a familiar time and place. The thick forest around me opened up above to a clear, blue sky. No clouds, just sun, and up ahead I could see a clearing. I took a step back, hoping to return, but I remained in this place. My body tensed, and I sensed a presence I could not fully discern. Committed now, I walked forward, hoping that Renée had chosen to follow me after all.

In the clearing, I saw an old well, made from large stones. A bucket rested next to the opening, and a long rope was coiled off to the side. A smell in the air attracted me—a beautiful and fragrant scent. I had never smelled anything like this before. The scent intoxicated me. I listened for a moment and could hear the birds chirping, far off, but the sounds seemed unreal and different somehow. When I began to walk around the well, butterflies popped up out of the grass, hundreds of them, their orange, brown and black filling my field of vision with clarity and deception.

"Good morning!"

He startled me. I whipped around and Henri stood behind me, dressed for the ball in his finest clothes, lute in hand. I stopped and wondered. His hair appeared tinged with silvery gray.

"How did you get here?" I asked.

"I am wondering the same thing." He picked a foot off the ground, looked at the sole, and then put it down again. "I was playing a song and then I was here."

He scratched his nose and then stopped, frozen. He heard something. A look of fear broke out on his face. He dropped the lute and raised his arms to protect his face.

"Leave me!" He screamed in terror, and the world shifted and turned dark.

I swayed, unstable, and the well remained planted in the center of my field of vision, but the clearing was gone, replaced with the Château's grounds. Far off, I could hear laughter and drunken revelry. The low, garden wall behind me, a stone bench, the place where Henri and I had kissed, and he had touched me.

"You, like this?" Henri had me in his arms. The terror on his face was replaced with lust. His hand groped me, and I saw insanity in his eyes. "You are in my domain now."

His face shifted, and I saw him. Through him, the fox rose up, teeth sharp and white, the snout, resplendent with silvery fur, his force outward and overpowering. This was no longer Henri, I had not been transported back in time. I struggled, yet he took me in his arms, and I wanted him off me. He laughed and shifted clean.

Tall, strong, and with pure magic he pressed me close to him, and I could feel him trying to absorb me into his spirit. Such power and confusion with no plan or purpose, just desire and insanity. The colors in his eyes and his hair, silver and long, soft and true. His face, shifting to animal, human and all. A true fey.

"Did I frighten you?" He wrapped his arms around me tight as his small foxy tongue licked my neck. "Did I?"

He breathed on me, and that fragrant smell opened me up, and I shivered in fear. I lost control and began to cry as he pushed past my barriers, ripping through my mind, seeing all.

His touch, like fire, was like Henri's, and my memories were torn from me. He used them against me and twisted them. His long nose jabbed at my cheek and his eyes were filled with madness and power.

"I'm coming for you. For you, for you, for you." His singsong voice, taunting me. "My little cinder girl, you better run, because I am coming for you!"

I fell back, stumbling against the well, and I covered my face, blocking out his voice from my mind. I kept falling into Renée's arms.

"Are you okay?" I did not know that she had been near me. She rubbed my hands and arms as I shivered without control.

I shook my head, unable to speak. His voice drifted away, and I tried to speak. I tried to say, "I saw him. I saw him."

Renée pulled forth her magic, shielding us, and she moved quickly, getting me to my feet. "Did you see the Silver Fox?"

"Yes. Yes, I did."

"What did he say?" Renée shouldered most of my weight and began half walking and half running us back to our cabin.

"He told me he is coming for me." My teeth chattered and I tried to say it again. "The Silver Fox is coming for me."

October 13

I have had some time to sleep, and Renée has been my constant companion. Our time in America has been short, and there is much to do, but with the fox after me, I chose to rest today. I do not often like to be pampered, but I stayed in bed most of the day. Late in the afternoon we talked about what had happened. I told her everything. I held nothing back, as I thought every bit of information she had would be useful. Maybe she could help me understand. When I finished, she grabbed our container of salt and she made a circle around each of our beds. We would need more. She worked fast, pulling our small beds close together in the center of the small cabin and then put the salt down. From her frantic movements, I could see she was frightened. For a woman who had stood up to the Queen and held her and all of her guards back with a word, she was so afraid, and I worried.

My magic is sound and strong, yet wild. I do not fully understand the power I have, and need practice and temperament, but now I do not have time on my side. He is coming for me. His presence is so strong and pervasive, flowing into me like water over the falls. He cannot be stopped.

When I look around while sitting on a chair in front of our cabin, I see a few men tend a fire, roasting some nuts. I can smell their flavor wafting my way. There is a chill in the air, as the season is changing, becoming colder at night. We are given food, have shelter, and the few other women here have shown us where to wash our clothes by the stream, and helped us by giving us freshly baked bread. We are starting to adapt to our life here as we plan what to do.

But I am afraid. We plan to head to another town, yet surely the fox will follow us. I suspect the glass slippers call to him no matter where we go. Renée and I talked as much as we could for today, and she is preparing our dinner as I write this. You will like her. She is a good woman. She loves fiercely and strong, not afraid to voice her opinions and to defend what she believes is right. Often she is quiet, watching yet not judging. She is wise as I would like to be one day. I can see why my mother loved her. I would have liked to have seen them together.

But it will be dark soon and I should stop writing. I am finding it hard to see in the fading light. I fear the oncoming night, for I wonder when the Silver Fox will return for me. Yet I long to write some more so that I can capture how I feel at this time. This day. This moment in time in which I had stepped out of the land of the fey back into this world. There's always such a joy that I feel in being aware that at this moment I can be open and free. No one can stop me from writing these words. The power that I have fills me with such joy as I just sit and let my mind wander. I have seen so much and sometimes, just sometimes, I like to enjoy life.

So much time has passed, and yet it hasn't. So much has changed, and yet it hasn't. Have I learned anything after all this time? I have learned that people are matchsticks that can be pushed and pulled and manipulated in, oh, so many ways. My little Cinder girl. Now that I am here there is so much to be seen and for me to do. You are filled with such knowledge and power but you have so much yet to learn. You are a young blossom, having seen the first light of day. With dew drops on your petals, you stumble out into the morning.

But I have come and I am in you. You are mine. I will dance with your limbs, frolicking in the light, swaying to the sound of the animals who sing for my delight. I will call forth and use your velvety voice and the long, blond hair that sways and blows in the soft, soft wind. Yet tonight, you are mine. I will take pleasure in you and having returned.

Write, write, write. All you want. You cannot escape me. I have come! Who am I? Who am I? Let me sing and tell you of my story. I am a King of the past and the future. Some have called me Lucifer (that Milton wrote me such a wonderful tale), Donatien Alphonse François or, as you might know him, Marquis de Sade. (Oh, I must digress as his mind is such a wonderful, tortured labyrinth of desire. I must visit him again soon. Maybe later tonight I will see him and then come back to you with what I have learned.) I will show you. We will have such wonderful times together. You and I.

Have you guessed it yet? Do you know me? Do you? Will you sing, sing, sing of who I am in the summer night or the morning rain? I like to play. I have fun with the world and all playthings. I am the Silver Fox who came to your mother as a young man. She longed and called to me in her loneliness as your father twittered away the hours working on his trade. I heard her call, came to her and loved her. For I am the despair in the night, but am also not quite light.

You cannot escape me. Run, run, run. How far can you? Will you cry, cry, cry and let me taste those little baby tears? It is too late for you, my dear. I have come! The Lord of foxes is here. I am here and I like you. You silvery thing. You little flit of a thing. My precious, pure woman. Let me see when you're raw, begging at my feet. I'll show you desire, ripped apart in time, with my spirit. No sense, no rhyme, my reason is all you'll ever need. I have come. It is too late for I am here. I am you and you are me. I am in you. For I am the Silver Fox, born when the sun was new and to die long after the sun closes his eyes for good. I am the Lord of the Fey, commander of the legions of sprites, pixies and faeries. Laughter and joy are my likes, but the spirits of War, Poverty, Pestilence and Insanity are my toys. Watch out, my gorgeous little thing! Watch out because I am here.

October 17

I am frightened. When I read my last entry, I ran to Renée, as I did not know what to do. I had no recollection of having written the passage. I stayed away from writing for the past few days because I needed to gather myself. Renée used a cleansing spell on me, and she could not detect any sign of him within me. He had gone. But I know he will return. The Silver Fox has come and gained control of me without my knowing. Renée has been teaching me as much protective magic as she can, and she is surrounding me with layers of natural protection. Salts and garlic and wards are all throughout our little home. But I know the truth—he will not be stopped. When he decides to come back for me, will I be ready? I detect no essence of him within me and I have read what he wrote through me several times, and I am afraid.

Renée has warned me that his power can break me easily, and she fears that I do not have the strength to stand up to him. At first, I was so scared, walking around wondering if I would lose my mind. The first night after he had come to me I went to sleep and had the oddest dream. I was lying in bed, and I turned over to see a beautiful young woman in my bed. Her eyes were a brilliant green, and the light from the morning sun shone on her face. Her eyes glowed with such brilliance, and I found solace in her. I realized that it was you, my beautiful and wonderful daughter. I am your mother, and your name came to me in that dream. I pulled you close and I kissed you on your forehead. Phoebe. Radiant and light. You looked to be all grown up in my dream, and I do not know how I recognized you, but I had met you for the first time, and a solidness formed around me. A wall of diamond that encircled us. As your mother, I needed to keep him away from you, and would need to protect you from harm.

My fear vanished, and in the dream I clothed myself with weaponry and power. I would not surrender without a fight, but how was I to know how to fight the enemy within? He had no physical form that I could see or interact with. He skipped through people, using and leaving us like discarded clothes. A shifter of personalities and sexes, that can come and go as he pleases.

I have come so far to be who I am. I will not be swayed or stopped. I realize that I am only one and that my strength is not enough to withstand the Fey Lord. But I must try. I know I need help, and Renée and I have begun enacting our plan. I do not know if it will work, but I am afraid that resistance itself is my only weapon. And for how long I can resist, I do not know.

Renée is calling me, and I must go. There is work to do.

October 19

After dinner tonight, I started to clean up and I felt an odd sensation within me. Mary, one of the women in the encampment, came over and asked if I felt sick. I sat back down at the table and felt it again. I put my hand over my belly and then she smiled.

"Did the baby move?" She put her hand on my shoulder.

"Yes, I felt a flutter inside." I put both hands on my belly and rubbed it.

I had felt you for the first time. My little Phoebe to be born of brilliance and light! I have been very busy for the last week, as there have been many preparations to be made. But tonight I sat down and wondered at the life within me. You fluttered around within me, alive with strength and purpose. I realized now that the home I would build for us would be needed in only a few months. Winter would be coming. The men in the encampment would be moving south to a warmer climate, and Renée and I would go with them.

They have agreed to allow us to come along, for we have paid them well with the King's coin. Gold is gold, and they committed to helping us. We will all in a few weeks head further south. I will sit in a wagon and watch as the world goes by, knowing that I bring Him with me. Renée and I have discussed the consequences of our departure with these people, but we need shelter, food and help. If we strike out on our own, we do not know whether we can survive the winter. Our best chance is to go with the people here, to remain part of a community, however small.

As you continue to grow within me, I promise to keep you safe. Now I understand more of what my mother must have felt when I was little. I am fiercely protective of you. My journey has been crooked and not clear, as I have traveled far only to realize who I am. I am no longer the little girl Princess who follows what she is told, spending time making plans and dreaming about the ball. That world and that life, that existence, is so far away now that I smile a bit thinking about it.

When he comes back for me, I will do all I can to stop him. If I could but speak to him or find common ground, maybe I could find a way to stop him. Yet perhaps I simply continue to be too innocent, perhaps he is who he is, and neither reason nor common ground, if that were even possible, will sway him. He enjoys madness and fun. And I am to be his toy.

I fear not for my safety but for yours. I must write this. I am a Chronicler, and it is my duty. If I do not survive this, I want you to know that I love you. I am your mother, your origin and guide. If I could teach you anything, and you would listen, it would simply be this: Love. Love with all your might. You will never regret it.

October 21

I've returned! Have you missed me? I do not see a feast laid out for me. Where are the flowers and wine and song? Am I not wanted? The little trinkets you left to ward against me are cute but I thought I told you last time that they will not work. You will learn. You will.

When you regain your senses, you will be far away from this rather boring waste of a place. But I've not much time today and as you and I will be seeing each other soon, I wish to speak more to Phoebe. She will one day grow up to read this and as I am not a monster (I'm a fey, a fox, sly and cunning yet not a beast). Though maybe a fox is a beast, but I think of beasts as something more. I am so slight and dainty like the sun shining through stained-glass, pick a shade of color. That's me there, depending on my mood.

Phoebe, dear, dear girl. You will be born in a few months' time and I can sense your power already in your little mamma's womb. You and your mother have a smell that I just adore. And it's not the fear. No, it's not that. One day you will grow up and I will watch you as I've watched your mother, and her mother before her. For years and years, I followed her progress watching her struggle. I'd check in from time to time to leave her hints about who she was. My paw marks could be found if she knew how to look and where. She'd always go out into the night, looking and searching with those glass slippers. She was pathetic at times, crying up to the heavens: "Please, please help me! Oh, fairy Godmother, come save me."

And so I did. Now she owes me. I waited many years for her to fall, but fall she did. Finally. For all she's done to keep me away, I'm going to play with her now and I want you to know that. I'll keep you safe as I need your help later, but I like playing these little games. Just yesterday I had a man jump off a cliff because he was so upset about his life. It was great fun feeling his terror but when he hit the ground, the light went out so quickly. His cracked head bled through and the fun is over too soon. But with your mother, if I don't hold back then I'll not have you. I'm tempted to try and break her to see if her magic would save her. I'm curious and I want to know. But I need you to do something great for me. Will you help? I do hope you will.

Please don't think me petty. I am the Silver Fox and I remember much. Never cross me, never turn your back on me and never, never, never forget me. For I will hunt you down, sniff you out and feed on your entrails like the animal I am. I'm taking your mother now and years from now when you see this page burned through with my magic it'll remind you that I owned her through and through. Then she and I will talk and I will give her three chances to help me. We shall see what see decides. But first, I want to show her my power. I'm off to have fun! As they say in the future, "Wish me luck!"

October 31

I have returned. Renée found me three days after the last passage. He had taken me in the woods and toyed with me. My right arm hurts and is bruised from him slamming it against a tree. He had abused and beaten me, and I am drained. I can see when he has control of me. I am able to watch from the inside but am unable to move my body. He controls me like a puppet, and there is nothing I can do. I do not yet understand why he wants me. I fear that I cannot protect you and all of the defensive words that Renée knows are useless against him. He has claimed me, and no matter how hard I fight him and resist I cannot break through.

Renée now sleeps with me, and she has asked the women of the encampment to help take turns watching over us. I do not know what he will do next or when he will return. I am so tired and need help. Please, do not let him come back.

But that's when I must come back! How can I resist such an invitation when you are so weepy and weak? You call to me and must I not oblige such a beautiful woman? I do apologize about your arm. I wanted to see what it would be like to change your skin color to black and blue as that shade suits you so much better. Maybe next time you'll not fight so hard to keep me away.

Yet I've come as I need your help and as you are the Chronicler and I'm just the crazy, little fox, we're going on a journey. I have a plan. Trust me, I do, and I'll share it with you soon. I'll be easy on you this time. I promise. Allons-y!

* * *

The dream began, and I woke up, grabbed a knife and stabbed poor Mary watching over us. She screamed, but the Silver Fox used me, and he flooded his power through my body. My left-hand, glowing brilliant white, opened a door, and we stepped through. I heard Renée calling me, but we had already gone. Now I am in the future and writing this passage, remembering what I am seeing. He is fey, and time for him is like a ball bouncing this way and that.

I am standing next to the King, and I can see the look of worry on everyone's faces. A map of Europe is on the table, sprawled out, marked with different colors. I can hear what they're saying, and then I see it, the Silver Fox playing with the tendrils of War, having them fall down all around. The First Consul is now the Emperor, and war is spreading like a disease across the land. The King is odd to me, and now I know why. I can see the fox, as me, standing behind him, whispering into his ear. Sweet nothings of Insanity have slithered down around the King, wrapped around his torso. The Silver Fox conducts the game and his mastery is complete.

"Come, let us move forward." He takes my hand, and we brush through time, and I see things I do not understand. The world is so changed. I see metal birds in the sky with people in them. I see tall buildings, and then he brings me to his masterpiece. War is now fought with powerful weapons that streak through the sky, and what he shows me horrifies me. I cannot tell you.

He pulls me faster, and the wave of dead fly under our feet. We stop in a far part of the world I have never seen or known to exist. We are up above a city, and then I see the flash. A great, holy light of the sun opens upon the earth, and people are burned away in a flash. The rumble and sound cuts through the sky, and in their tracks people become ash as their shadows are fused to the sides of their houses.

And then I realize that I am powerless against him. He is like a god and I, so small and without power, can never win. He cannot be stopped. I realize the truth. I can see it in the hearts and minds of the men and women we fly over. I see it. There is always someone who wants to join him. There is hatred, and people want revenge. They call him to their heart, and he gives them what they want. In return, he takes great pleasure out of the suffering he sees. And I? I am lost. I am a little girl whom he wants to drive mad. But why? Why does he toy with me so?

November 4

Renée has tied me to a chair, but my left arm is free so that I can write. I do not know how many days have passed. How can we defeat someone who can be everywhere and do anything? What am I to do? I feel ashamed and out of control. I am fighting him. I am trying my best, but…

What? It's not working? Don't like the fact that I can just pop in and that all will be okay. You are mine now. Don't ever forget that. Let me tell you a story about your future. Many years from now your story will be told to millions of children around the world. And do you know what they'll remember? They're going to remember that you were a poor little girl who had nothing and that you were mistreated by your stepmother and stepsisters. Poor little you! But then, one day, your

Faerie Godmother comes and helps you get the Prince who rescues you from your miserable little situation.

Isn't that funny? That's what people will remember you for. Not for anything else but that you became a Princess and lived happily ever after. Isn't that wonderful?

I will fight you. I will not let you win. I will. I will. I will.

Feel better now, do you? I'm going to take you on a journey. Renée has never truly explained to you what your powers are, has she? It is time that you understood what I want from you and how you can help me. Remember, you are a Chronicler of events. You can see them and capture them in your mind and share with others what you know and have seen, but there's so much more for you to learn. Once you learn what you can do with your power, then we'll see if you'll fight me any longer. Ready, set and here we go!

The journey is straight
the road is long
Where, oh where, has
My pretty girl gone?

* * *

I woke up lying in bed. I was untied, and from the window streams of the morning sun shone in, but it was quiet. The room looked different, and as I came out of my deep slumber I realized that I was somewhere else. I had never been in this bed before.

For a moment, I listened to the sound of birds calling outside. Early morning, and I would guess autumn. The smell of fresh baked bread came wafting in from another room. I rubbed my eyes, yawned and then stretched a bit.

When I shifted my legs, I stopped. My left thigh had grazed a wet spot in the bed. I tried to sit up but was weak. I placed my hand under the covers and felt the spot. My heart raced and I looked at my hand, seeing blood. I threw the sheet off of me and called for Renée. My undergarments were saturated, and the cold, sticky feeling frightened me. I called for Renée again, and I could hear movement from the other room as she rushed to come to me.

I could not get up out of bed. I tried, but fatigue kept me there. My hands looked so pale. I put my hands on my belly and could not feel you. Were you hurt? Did I lose you? Shifting into the morning light, I focused and called on my power. My hand began to glow, and I fell back onto the pillow. I had no strength.

Renée came running into the room and I looked over at her—and saw the Silver Fox. He had dressed himself in her clothes and he was carrying a large, metal pot.

"Oh my, are you okay?" His sing-song voice tried, badly, to mimic Renée's voice.

I wanted to hit him.

He smiled and barely contained his laughter. "Is there anything wrong, my dear?"

Again, I wanted to slap him, knocking his foxy look off his face. His face changed, and his feral side showed through and then faded back off into the background.

I tried to talk but could not. He came closer, hair pulled back like Renée's, and as he stood next to me, he tilted the metal pot onto the bed and blood flowed out onto my legs.

"Haven't had enough pig's blood? I've plenty for you."

His laughter cracked, and he threw the metal bowl across the room and could not stop laughing. He kept laughing until a coughing fit caught him, and he choked for a bit on his own fun.

"Why are you doing this to me?"

He fell onto the bed and propped himself up on his elbows. "Because, because, because—I can."

I shut my eyes and listened. I was in a dream, within a dream, dreaming about a dream. His power, thick over me, pulled me back, and I opened my eyes.

"What would you do if you lost your daughter?" He pulled himself up and then sat on the bed next to me. His hands were covered in the pig's blood. Brushing away the hair from my eyes, he asked, "What would you do?"

How could I answer? What could I say? I fought, in my mind, but he remained. I tried to shut him out from my soul, but could not. His power captured me whole. I began to cry. My body was wracked in pain, so I released my fear and fell into my sorrow.

He took pity on me and held my hand in his own. "It is time for you to understand why I need you. I have broken you enough and want you to understand how you can use your powers to help me."

I sobbed and listened with no will of my own left. He had stripped me down and held all the power over me that should have been mine.

"I want you to save your mother's life for me." He said the words with reverence and waited to see if I had heard him.

"Did you hear me?" He held my chin in his hand and wiped the tears from my face.

I nodded in fear, as I knew not what he would next do to me.

"Renée hasn't fully told you about your powers to change history. Now I will bring you to three key moments in your life. What you decide to change or not change is up to you, except when I call for you to help me save your mother. Then, if you do not obey me, I will take Phoebe from you." He patted back my hair and his face changed again, his fox snout so close to my cheek that I could smell his breath. "I will let you go now so that you can rest. But soon I will come back for you."

I closed my eyes to hide from him, and he disappeared, leaving me to my sobs and fear.

November 7

Renée and I have talked. The moments that I remain me are harder to find. I can see it in her eyes, as she wonders whether I am still me or if he possesses me. She is afraid that I will hurt someone or myself. I am in my room and am again tied to the chair. Renée told me that I had to be secured because I had run off and tried to hurt myself. She is worried for me, I can see it in her face and I do not know what I can do.

How do you win against this insanity? I have talked and talked, but Renée has not been able to help save me. I am powerless and alone. No, that is not true. I am filled with sorrow. He will come back soon. He has not left me alone for more than a few days. I told Renée what he wants, and she fears that his request will break the natural order, but I have no sense of how to do his bidding, even if I did wish to do so.

I remember my mother's smile. I pray for that now. I pray to understand what he wants from me and that she will come to me and fill me with light. A light that will cleanse me and bring me back home and fill me with peace.

November 11

As our little Cinder girl is taking a nap, let me try and entertain you. I'm not such a bad man. Well, I'm not a man. I'm a fey and a fox who's a flighty little thing. I am the West and the East, and, well, I can see you don't care. What do you care about? What do you do if you could be what you want to be? Like me, in a tree, with the sea, let me take a—well, let's not go there or I'll be off wandering down memory lane and you'll not listen to me.

You're not like your mother, are you? I like the dark I see in you. It is shades of nightfall and twilight in your eyes. She will never surrender to me and be mine and maybe that's why I've stayed so long as she won't give in. She'll fall apart and then I'd lose you and I don't want that now, do I? Help convince her to give me what I want. Will you do that for me? Think on it.

Let me go now. You need your rest as does your mother. She is me and I am her as we are like each other. Take care of her and I'll be back soon. I will. I promise. Goodnight my sweet little one. Goodnight.

November 13

Renée has told me that it is cold outside. I do not remember the last time I was out. I have been here, in this room, tied to the chair for a long time. I am fed, and she has washed and clothed me. I have hours that I am at peace and we go for walks, and then I am brought back to this room. She told me that I keep changing into him and that she is afraid that I might hurt someone. When I am calm, like this, I try to not think of what has happened to me. The outer world has fallen away, and all I have now are these times. I do not remember when he takes over. I do not wish to talk more about this.

Soon it will be the time to enact our plan. The two of us are going to leave the encampment, and we will not be near any people so that I cannot hurt anyone. With my magic so strong and raw, Renée is afraid that I might surrender and use my powers for him.

I am going now. I do not know when I will be able to write next. Maybe there is a chance that I might lose myself entirely and, if I do, I want you to know that I love you. It is all I can say as a mother right now. I will fight for you, and I will not give up. But nothing I have done so far has worked. Nothing I have tried to do to stop him matters or even appears to have a chance of working. But I will not give up. I will keep trying. But for now, I just want some rest. I love you.

November 21

I am beginning to be bored with you. You resist me still. Your friend watches over you night and day, but her magic cannot stop me. Let me take you to your first chance. Let us return and see. I think I shall have some fun with this. And try not to be so glum, I have waited a long time for this. You could at least give me the satisfaction of playing along. Can you try and pretend to care?

I am not all evil. I am erratic and, oh, well you should know by now. I dote on you my little dove. Trust me, I do. Come with me, come back, come to the beginning and let us see what you will do. Remember, you are a Chronicler and can change history. You must learn how! But, enough of that, let us go and travel back there. Now.

* * *

I opened my eyes and squinted. My head hurt and around me people danced, twirling around. I wore my beautiful blue gown, and my glass slippers were on my feet still. In the large room, I caught a glimpse of Clarissa dancing and laughing. I had traveled back. A young attendant came to me and asked me for my name. I told him and waited to be announced. Two women were in front of me with their family. I stood alone with no one to support me. My palms sweated and I took a deep breath, held it and slowly exhaled. The dress made me look truly beautiful, but it was tight around my waist. I would be happy to be changed in a few hours.

I listened as the family in front of me was announced, and polite clapping filled the hall. The young attendant waved me forward, and I took a few steps more into the room. He blew a few notes from his trumpet and called out to the gathering of nobles, "From the west, we are honored tonight by Miss Sophia."

My name meant nothing to any of them. I walked forward and my shoes shot out sparks of blue that whipped around me, little faerie lights, dancing around my dress. I strode forward with purpose, and heads turned to see my dress flow with power and might. Magic crackled around me and my entrance into society drew many an eye. I had always thought the magic that night had come from my Fairy Godmother. I knew better now. The clothes, coach and shoes were given to me by the wily fox, but the rest was mine.

I could see people whispering to each other as I passed by, and with purpose I walked to the center of the room toward the Prince. People gave way, and blue lights swirled around me, like tiny fireflies, dancing in delight.

A gentleman talking with the Prince nodded in my direction and then he turned around. I remember this moment. This is when it all happened and became real to me. I was Sophia still. My stepsisters had yet to poison people with their tales of my working for them, cleaning up their messes and their lies about me. Before the time that everyone called me Cinderella. I was at the moment of innocence, and all would fall together.

"I am enchanted to meet you this fine evening." The Prince took my hand and kissed it with such charm.

I wore light blue gloves and could not feel his lips on my skin, but a shiver went through me, nonetheless, and a small part of me thrilled inside. "I am delighted to meet you, too."

He smiled, and the night turned to day for me. My heart beat faster, and I wanted him to kiss me again. His eyes appeared to twinkle, and the blue energy that swirled around me intensified, and those nearest us took a step back in concern.

"Who are you?" His simple question asked more than the words.

"I am a merchant's daughter." I lowered my head, glanced away for a moment and needed to rally. I was talking to the Prince. I needed to make my mark. This was my moment. "I feel a bit lost as this is my first ball."

"I will take care of you then. You will be my guest." He put out his arm for me to take hold of. "Would you like to dance?"

A circle of interested people had surrounded us. I had not noticed them before, but the Prince had. He saw the attention we were getting and he liked it.

I hesitated for a moment and then took his arm. He smiled again and then pulled me close to him. Raising his arm, he made a quick motion with his hand and the music commenced. He pulled me with him across the dance floor, and I could not take my eyes off of him. I must admit that I could not do so. He was so charming that night. What had happened to us?

I never wanted the dance to end. He covered up all my mistakes, leading me with expertise and precision. As we danced, we flowed across the floor, and my magic surrounded us in light and crackling energy. We were a spectacle to behold. The Prince and a young magical woman—not a common sight of the day.

The music swelled, and we danced along, our eyes locked. I could tell that neither of us wanted the song to end. For that moment, we were caught in each other and our spirits were entwined and happy. Happy with the possibilities of what we could do together as a couple, as two who would fall in love.

When the song ended, I expected him to bow and leave me for another, as I could see the other girls lining up in a circle, waiting to see whom he would choose next. I could see the anxiety on their faces, and I realized that I had been picked above them all. How they must have hated me with my magic dress and shoes. They all looked glorious to me, but how could they compete with my magic? They simply could not.

I went to pull away from him and he leaned closer and asked, "Would you like another?"

And I did. I wanted to dance the rest of my life with him. How foolish I was, but I fell for him there with his wavy hair, accepting smile and firm hands. The hands of a Prince never rough or showing the sign of working the land. My own hands were chapped from having scrubbed and washed the entire house in the anticipation that one of my stepsisters would be chosen by him. How laughable my situation was! How extraordinary that I could be twirling in my blue dress, which shot off sparks like fire, with the Prince.

He twirled me and I spun, spun, faster and faster into his awaiting arms, and we came together as though it was our destiny. I remember all this. Reliving it again, with the memories I now have was private and special. We danced for hours, and slowly the onlookers gathered round, judging me without having heard me speak a word. Many were jealous and put off by my arrival and with how easily I stole the Prince's heart.

At an intermission, he pulled me away to a balcony. He smiled and went over to a table, pouring me a glass of wine.

"Here, you look thirsty."

I accepted and took a tiny sip. The dancing and the closed quarters with so many people had exhausted me. I had been working since before the dawn, scrubbing away, but tired or not, I would not let my fatigue show.

"Thank you."

I put my glass down and looked up at the full moon, not quite certain where the conversation should go.

The Prince poured himself a glass and took a sip, looking at me with great interest. Now I know what that look meant, but at such a young age I took his staring at me as simple curiosity. Back in the large hall, I could hear the low rumble of all the guests as they laughed and talked during the intermission.

"What is your name?" He stood by me and leaned against the balcony like a sly cat.

"Did you not hear me being announced when I came in?"

He nodded. "Yes, I did but I want to hear you say it."

"My name is Sophia, Your Highness." I curtsied and kept my eyes low.

"Sophia, the cinder girl." He mumbled it low and when he said my name, a thrill passed through me.

A moment in time was coming quickly. A path in the road and I realized that I would need to make a decision. I remember what I had done when this happened the first time. How my life had changed from that moment onward. I glanced up at the sky and could see a few stars and the bright moon, climbing into the sky. My gown flowed around me and the magic within rested a bit. All was calm.

The quiet moment continued between us and I did not know what to say.

"Sophia, come kiss me." The Prince put down his glass and then put both hands, palm down, on the balcony. He leaned against the stone, waiting.

My choice, the thoughts that circled all through my head, and my heart beat like fire thrumming to the dawn of a new day. I could turn toward him, or I could leave. I know what I had done before, but now, with all that I knew and everything that we had been through, would I choose different? All the pain and the hurt, his harsh words and criticism and yet, here, in the dark of the night, with music swelling from the ball, I looked into his eyes and he wanted me. I could see it now. He wanted me like a man wanting a drink in the dessert, and I could deny or surrender to him.

Would my life be different if I made a change now? Why had the Silver Fox brought me here? There had to be a reason. There always was with him. It was a game within a game, yet could I erase all of my history by walking away or declining his request?

I acted and quickly came forward, kissing him on the cheek, but this time, I went further and with gentle care I closed his eyes with my hand and kissed him on the lips, lingering for a moment so that he could take my presence all in.

Then I withdrew, hovering over his lips for an instant longer, and I pulled back with fiery intent. He opened his eyes and I could see that I had surprised him. He took a breath and then coughed into his hand. He regained his composure and I could see him thinking on what to do next. I had changed the rules and made a slight change in history. What would he say and do?

"Thank you." He came away from the balcony and put out his arm. "We should get back to the ball."

"Let us go back and dance some more." I accepted his arm. "I would like that."

When we entered the room, all chatter ceased, and the guests turned to us, whispering. We had been gone for only a few minutes, but I suspect the rumors had already begun. That was the way of court life. In the past, when I did this for the first time, the attention and the onlookers overwhelmed me. I leaned close to the Prince and he protected me. Yet tonight I held my head high and smiled right at the faces in the crowd. They were powdered, primped and jealous. I smiled openly and let my warmth flood out over the group.

The Prince raised his arm and shouted for all to hear, "Let us have music and dance!"

The music struck up instantly and we skipped across the floor and I laughed, loving every moment. For the rest of the night, we danced and my magic flared, sending blue shocks of light spinning around us, harmless yet awe-inspiring. Magic so rare and often not seen, the bewildered guests gave us some privacy, as no one dared enter into my sphere of influence for fear that the sparks would hit them.

I cannot remember how many songs we danced together, but another break came and I could see that midnight was upon me. Once again, I had nearly forgotten. At the end of the song, I begged away so I could attend to myself, but, like before, he could not be so easily fooled.

He pretended to laugh at a joke of mine and then whispered into my ear. "You are leaving, are you not?"

I would not lie to him. For all that we had gone through, I did not wish to plant a seed of untruth between us.

"Yes, I must leave for the night. It is nearly past my time."

He walked me to a side room and we were alone once inside. "Is there nothing I can say to make you stay for one more dance?"

"No, I must go."

He thought a moment, started to speak, and stopped. A moment passed and he asked, "Will I see you again?"

I could answer with such accuracy now. "Yes, you will if you want to."

"You are so cryptic and mysterious."

I came close to him, tip-toed and gave him a kiss on the lips. "No, I am not. I simply speak the truth."

He marveled at my words and pulled me close, giving me a deep kiss of wonder. Young love, so warm and true and heartfelt! I allowed him to kiss me and returned his affection. We stood pressed against each other as best we could, as my gown acted as a guardian for me, keeping us somewhat separated. The kiss lasted longer than I had remembered and much more passionate as the years stretched by and all of my memories and love fell into that simple act.

I counted the seconds in my head and there I was, like a girl again, kissing the Prince, falling in love again and knowing that the future would bring me such pain and hurt. He was a man and, for him, he gave his heart so easily and without regret. As a woman, trust took time and was much more private and unspoken. The words that he would say to me about his love would be like poetry that he wanted the world to see, whereas I would simply show him my love for years, and years and years. My love would be a ribbon stretched through time, a gift of sight, sound and experience, and yet he would one day reject it.

Having to do it all over again, foolish, foolish me! I would choose love. Because it is right, it is true, it is.

The clock struck midnight and a flurry of angst washed over me. I would change back to myself and needed to go. I had learned. Given a choice to change the past, I stayed true to my heart and my belief in love. The clock struck twice, and I pulled away from him. He looked confused as men often do when you stop kissing them, wondering what they had done wrong, when it was not what they were doing then but what they had already done or would do in the future.

"Goodnight, my Prince."

"Why do you go?" He held on to me.

"So you will come find me." I pulled away and then stopped. The clock struck thrice. I wanted to do something different. I wanted to break through and leave a mark. I truly do not know why, but I wanted to give him one more chance.

I leaned forward and took two fingers and touched his forehead. "If you would love me, then do it. Truly, with all your heart, do it. Be true to me."

I shifted for him and he saw me as I am now. I was breaking all the rules and transformed in front of him. The clock struck four. I aged in front of him and he pulled back, confused and unsure as to what was happening. I willed it and my gown vanished and he saw me as I am now with my simple clothing, long hair, pregnant and several years older. I lost count of the chimes.

"Goodbye." I turned around to go.

"How will I find you?" He looked distraught.

"Follow your heart." I slipped out of my glass slippers and left one on the floor. I bent down and took the other in my hand. He stared at me with such amazement and wonder, like having seen life for the first time in all its glory and beauty. He saw me as I was, and I wanted to stay, but the game was up. The time had passed. I had made my choice.

I turned and ran. Over my shoulder I glanced and saw him bend down to pick up the glass slipper. He caressed it and I wondered. Would he change?

* * *

I awoke with a start, reached for my feet yet still wore my glass slippers. All had been a dream, yet parts had been real. Looking around, I did not recognize my surroundings. I lay in bed, and the room around me was filled with white. Next to me the Silver Fox rested with his eyes closed. His white hair, brushed and pulled back into a ponytail and the morning light shone on part of his face. He looked innocent and somewhat at peace.

A bird outside began to chirp and his one eye opened, staring back at me. "Good morning, my Chronicler."

Wary, I propped myself up in bed and asked, "What do you want with me?"

"I am impressed with your abilities and must admit that you handled yourself well with the Prince." He rubbed his eyes and yawned. "Interesting choice. You still chose him and didn't change your history. I'm surprised."

He kicked his feet off the end of the bed and jumped up, stretching far to the ceiling. For a moment, he shifted and I could see the fox in him.

"Will you please take me home?"

"No, but I will answer your first question." He glanced around the room in an absent-minded way and mumbled, "Where did I put the tea?" He fell to his knees and pulled a tray from underneath the bed. On it were some bread, cheese, strawberries and a pot of tea.

He offered me some, and I accepted as I could not remember when I last had my fill. With bread crumbs tumbling onto the front of his shirt as he wrestled with a piece of bread, he said, "Do you know that I loved your mother so?"

"She told me a story about you, but I thought it a fable."

"No, I am real and for years your mother and I would meet at night and be together in the land of the Fey. I wanted her to come join me forever and become my bride, but she refused as she did not wish to abandon you." He put his piece of bread down and poured himself a cup of tea. The steam rose toward the ceiling and he kept quiet.

I leaned forward, prepared to fight him and asked, "Did you kill my mother?"

"Kill her? My dear Cinder girl, no!" He put the cup down and knelt by the side of the bed and held my hand, his face so close to mine that I backed away in fear. "I loved your mother. We loved each other and she was taken away from me and died."

"If you love her, then why are you torturing me?" I pulled away from him.

"I wasn't always like this. And now I need you to help me bring her back."

"Bring her back? She has been dead for more than 12 years now!"

He laughed and shook his head. "You do not understand as you are not fully fey. Time is an ebb and flow. At times, I feel as eternity has passed since Justine has died, and yet sometimes, it's as though she just left me." He moved away from me and sat back down in his chair. "I waited for you to learn of your power, but you didn't. I waited as you suffered under your stepmother, thinking she would be the one to force your magic to blossom, but again, you did not. Finally, I saw a spark in you after you met the Prince, but nothing I tried could awaken the power within you. So I waited."

"If I knew how to use all of my power, I would cast you out." I spit at him and missed.

"Feisty, aren't you, in the morning?" He grinned and showed me his fox teeth. "For you years passed, but still I waited, thinking that if I helped you as your Fairy Godmother that you would become your mother's daughter and your powers would awaken. Yet again, you did not."

"Truly, what do you want from me?"

"I already told you. I just don't know if you'll do it." He put his arms out in front of him, imploring me. "I want you to bring back your mother."

I watched him with distrust. "You tell me only half the truth."

"You are very perceptive." He leaned back in his chair and his arms fell at his side. "You will have to figure the rest out yourself."

He winked at me and was gone.

* * *

The room shifted and I fell a long way in a deep, deep sleep. When I woke, I was in a cave and a small fire was at the opening. Outside it was snowing. I was cold. I had several blankets on me and as I oriented myself I tried to sit up and grunted. Renée heard me and came to my side. She held a bowl of warm broth and helped me sit up.

The snow came down softly outside and blew gently from a light wind. The trees looked magical as they were covered in the light fluff. I drank some of the broth and accepted a piece of hard bread.

"How are you feeling?" Renée touched my forehead and then eased back to sit beside me against the cave's wall.

"A bit disoriented." I pulled the blankets tightly around me and shivered. "How long have I been gone?"

"A full day." Renée offered me more broth and I accepted.

We sat in silence for a few minutes as I continued to sip the broth. The fire crackled and I looked down, saw the glass slippers still on my feet and then saw my hand glowing with a faint sheen of phosphorescence. I stopped and held up my hand. Renée watched me but kept quiet.

"Why is my hand glowing?" I stopped drinking and put the bowl down. I looked around the cave and saw piles of clothing, stores of food and my books. The most recent one glowed in the same light.

Renée took my hand and squeezed it. "You are a Chronicler. An extremely powerful one."

I did not understand. Renée said, "Do not worry about your magic right now. We must plan on how to defeat him."

I let it go. How long the Silver Fox would leave me alone was unknown to me. He could return at his whim. I needed to eat and rest so I could build up my strength.

I took another bite of the bread and while chewing asked, "What am I going to do?"

"If you do not break his hold on you, you will be lost to us and will join him forever in the faerie world."

I dipped a piece of bread into the broth. "Do you want to know what happened to me?"

"No, I need not know." She pointed over to the books. "You are a Chronicler. Everything's being written. If I need to know, I can follow along."

I started to ask a question, but Renée held up her hand. "You are being tested with your powers and you were tempted to stay. The Silver Fox preys not only on your weaknesses but your hopes and dreams."

"I have tried to stop him. When he comes for me, there is nothing I can do to win against him."

"Exactly." Renée smiled and reached for my glowing hand and it went dark.

November 23

I am back writing after having rested. I have paged back through my diary and can see the dreams that I have lived through. It is all written down—even the Silver Fox's words through me. He is coming back for me. I can feel it. I know that he will turn his eye back to me, and I do not have much time. The time that I do have I want to spend it with you. My beautiful daughter. My child and light. One day I hope you will find my books and that you will learn of me and be happy.

The early snow covered the ground, and I went for a walk yesterday with Renée. We have left the encampment and are on our own. Renée feared that I might hurt someone when I was not myself and the men wanted me far away as they saw me as a bad omen. Our moving here is for the best. There is a local tribe of Indians we met yesterday, and they are willing to trade with us and have offered assistance. With winter approaching, we will need their help to survive.

I think back about my last dream state with the Silver Fox and wonder. Did I really live through meeting the Prince again? I wonder if he is searching for me as I asked him to do. Or, is everything only in my imagination and I am alone still and been forgotten? There was a time when I used to look at the Prince and admire him, and how I loved him with all of my soul. But our years together, have changed us, and yet a part of me still wishes that we could be happy.

Yet I did not change the past and decide not to be with the Prince as I could have. Instead, I allowed history to happen as it ought, but I had to try by asking him to come for me. I wondered if he had changed and become a better man if I would be with him still. What would I do if I saw him walking up over the small hill, coming through the trees toward this cave? And then I laugh, as the Prince I know would never live in a cave, for this dream I have created of him does not exist.

I am surprised by how much I wanted him to come for me and to change. When I awoke in the cave, I expected him to be there—to have traveled the world, looking for me as I am his one true love. When we first met, I thought our love would transcend time and distance and that he could pinpoint me on any map because his heart could feel mine. I believe in love, and always will, but love is not magic.

When I realized that the Prince had not found me, I wondered if he was lost somewhere, fighting the ocean's powerful waves and this elaborate story took shape in my mind. But the truth was much simpler. Much, much easier to tell and understand. The Prince chose to stop loving me and had moved on. There is no faerie tale ending to the story.

And what of your father, my once bright and glorious Henri? I still do not wish to write about him. I need more time to heal my heart. I have not spoken to Renée about these thoughts and feelings as they are private, and as long as my magic holds strong only you can see these passages. What you choose to do with these words of mine is for you to decide.

My time runs short. I know that. I sense his attention turning back and he will thrust all his power on me. yes, i am coming—for you. I will resist him as long as I can. I will. But in the time that I have remaining, I want to tell you what I have learned.

When I realized that the Prince would not be scouring the world looking for me and that Henri had chosen my friend over me, I understood. Do not let love rule you. No man (or woman) can complete you. I have looked, most of my life, for someone to save me, but, in the end, only I can do it. Stop! This is the only secret you need to know. Love yourself. All else will follow. it's too late. i have come!

* * *

I am back. And it appears not a teensy weensy moment too soon. I've played with you nicely for the last few times, but now I'm going to take you on an adult ride. We're going to have some fun together. Just you and I like old friends, but we're not. I want—what do I want? Maybe I should think on that for a second. There, got it. I want you to fall. What happens when our pretty princess scuffs her knees? When you fall down and hit the ground hard? Will you give up? Then, will you help me?

What will you do when I twist you in two, tearing your mind apart? I'm curious. When you're facing the abyss, will you still be singing your praises about Love? Love, love, love. If love is what you want, then let's see what you do with it. Let us go, down the path, through the fields, over the hill to where your past is waiting for you and… a little something else.

* * *

I was running but I did not quite know why. So I stopped and rested for a moment. The moon hung low on the horizon and a summer breeze cooled me.

"Do you think we ran far enough away?" Henri turned back around and listened for anyone you might have followed us.

"I do not see anyone coming this way." I looked at his profile in the moonlight and my resolve quickly faded.

We had run through the Château's gardens, and I sat on a stone bench to catch my breath. Henri paused for a moment, staring back through the maze of bushes and decided we were safe. No one would find us this far from the revelry.

"I would play for you, but I fear our friends would find us." He gently put down the lute and lingered for a moment, resting his hand on it as though he were saying a tiny prayer. I knew what he hoped for and he need not pray.

I looked up at the moon and, out of the corner of my eye, watched him sit down on the bench next to me. The moon, a crescent, hung low, casting a dim light over us. Tonight was a perfect night for fun and love. A night that I could make into whatever I desired. Clarissa had run off with the rest of those at the ball, lost in drink and debauchery. She had given herself fully to the spirit of the night but I had more specific plans.

"Can we not talk, please?" I reached for his hand and held it.

He nodded and then turned toward me, putting his right hand on the back of my neck, pulling me toward him into a full kiss of warmth that tingled and excited me. How long had it been since I had kissed someone new? The Prince's kisses, in the beginning, were full of passion yet still tender. Over the years, as he strayed, they changed in intensity, frequency until he often did not kiss me, performing only his duty to try and produce an heir.

Tonight, I could be whoever I wanted to be. Away from my homeland, my husband partaking in the local delicacies back in England, so why should I remain true to him?

I leaned into Henri's kiss and I let go of his hand, feeling his back and then running my hand through his hair. The thickness of it, the smell of him and the taste of his youth on my tongue awakened me. He could teach me much, but I, a married woman with no child, what could I offer him? Inside, I unlocked the door and allowed myself to feel alive for the first time in years. I heard myself sigh and I pulled away from the kiss, looking into his face. His eyes, perfect, and his mouth so wanting and full of desire. I froze the moment in time. This was my decision point. I could pull back, as he expected, or I could go down a different path and break my oath and dip into the night of bliss to be lost, for this moment, forever in this moment, to be free and myself.

He waited, having agreed not to speak, hesitant to push me as he knew enough about the ways of love to not be a rake, forcing himself on me. He could see in my face the internal struggle and then he tipped the balance. He smiled at me, open and pure, holding back, but having shown me enough that his confidence would win him the night. And it did.

But now in this second reliving, I waited for just a moment longer and weighed the consequences in my mind. I realized that what I was about to do would lead me to where I am in the present. I am pregnant, Henri has abandoned me, and I am alone. I have been rejected, and Henri's love for me is not true or constant. He wanted me, but now he has tossed me aside, and all that I have given to him is for naught. With my magic, I have a choice. The temptation of it rose up inside as I realized that I could change the past and stop the hurt by refusing Henri. I simply had to turn my face away and play shy. Now I understood and saw the truth to the Silver Fox's test for me. If I could change my own past and vanquish the pain and undo what I had given to Henri, would I?

But I am too weak. I returned Henri's smile and I leaned closer to him and simply said, "Yes."

He took my face in his hands and said, "No matter what I do and how I act you can always trust me."

I took his words and wrapped them close in my heart. I believed him.

Now I still need him as I would a crutch or some need wine. Any chance to be with him, I would take. Even to relive what I knew would become hurtful for me, yes, I would choose the same. And I did.

Henri's smiled widened, and he accepted my kiss. I opened my heart to him. I poured all my love, my desire and needs into him. I lost myself in that moment and he, a careful and giving lover, returned the feeling. Connected in spirit, we kissed and his hand glanced across my breast, testing the waters, but I did not deflect him. Tonight I would be open and true, losing myself to the world. The intensity of the kiss increased, and I wanted him. I wanted to hold him, love him and feel him, knowing that he would betray me and that I am weak and still needed him. My heart ached, and the pain swelled within me so that the tears rose up within me, and I could not withstand the hurt any longer.

"No!" I raised my left hand and basked in its fiery light. I stood up seeing a glimmer of myself remain with Henri, and I willed the scene to change—and the universe listened.

The Silver Fox appeared next to me, hiding his expression and remained passive. "Do you see now?"

"That time between Henri and me is my secret, and you cannot have that." I stood defiant before him and ready.

"I like the spirit in you. I truly do." His smile frightened me. His face shifted into more of a fox, and I could see his teeth in the moonlight. "Just like your mother. But look over there, and tell me what you see."

I turned and saw a long, dark passage in the castle, and I did not want to walk down it. I knew where he had brought me. He stood back and said nothing.

With surety of what I would find, I stepped forward with determined slowness, and my heart raced. I would see Henri again. I came alive and walked into the room and there he sat, waiting for me. This was the last time I saw him. Perhaps I could change what happened between us.

"You have come to say your goodbye?" His tone like steel.

175

"I have come to ask for forgiveness and to apologize for cursing you." I ran to him and knelt by his feet. "Please, I had become angry at you and I was wrong."

He shifted his body away from me. "You poisoned my mind and I cannot forgive you for that."

"Can you not see how angry I was as you were with Clarissa?" I reached for his knee and held on tightly.

"I see that you used your witch's power to try and destroy my mind." He cast my hands off of him. "Are you finished?"

"But Henri, please! I am pregnant with your child. We can be happy together in time. I will come back to you again after you have had time to forgive me. Please!" I supplicated myself before him, low on the ground.

"I want nothing to do with you." He leaned down and grabbed my face in his hands. "I cast you out of my heart and mind. Do you not see that I simply wanted some enjoyment and you were willing?"

His words hurt like arrows that pierced into me. I cried and could not stop. He pushed me away and said, "Take your witch's magic and demon child with you and leave me. I do not love you."

"But what of all the times we had? How can you say this?"

"I am young and must be allowed to make mistakes as the young do." He did not hide the disgust in his eyes. "And you were my mistake. Goodbye."

I fell back and cried. "Please, please don't leave me! I would do anything for you." My mind raced, and I knew the next words I would say, but again, change them I could, but I chose not to. "Stay with Clarissa, I will not say a word. But please, remember me for a time and come to me, too. Please, do not forget me!"

He stood up and spit on the floor next to me. "I will have none of you."

He walked away from me, and I knew he would be gone forever. Yet now, I had the power to burn his mind with my hurt and fury. I wanted to give in to my anger. When he wanted me, I gave him all. I loved him, laughed, listened and longed to be with him as he was my night and day. All along, he had simply used me to fill up the time when he was lonely and now he had moved on, using what I had done to him as a means to escape with ease. He had flitted on to his next conquest, allowing himself to be free of responsibility and consequences.

He once had told me to trust him and I, a foolish girl, believed him. Now his selfishness angered me. How could he desert me so truly? He had not even one kind word for me. And he saw himself as right, true and could not see how hurtful he treated me. All was meant for him as it was easier that way. Never could he look in the mirror and admit how he used people, tossed them aside and then moved on, flitting like a butterfly in the sun, drinking from flower to flower and never resting long. Never.

The power I had within my veins would allow me to rewrite history, to change the past, but I could not change how he had treated me. I wanted him to want me and he did not. He left the room and I sobbed, loudly and hard, on the floor. My vision blurred, he came beside me and knelt down and offered me his hand. I accepted and the Silver Fox pulled me close.

"Not so easy, is it?" He said nothing else and held me in his arms, making soothing noises to help calm me.

Time passed, and the room in the castle faded away. I noticed that he was dressed in the best finery. He helped me up, and we walked away from the past, seeing it fade away, and our world dropped beneath us and for several moments we floated through the Land of the Fey crossing the tops of flowers, being so small, and yet when we arrived where he wanted me to be the world had changed yet again. I did not recognize our surroundings. My hand still glowing, I remained cautious and prepared to defend myself, but the kindness on his face remained.

I wondered, back in the real world, what did Renée see of me? I did not know, but she would protect me as best she could. I could trust in her.

"Do you know where you are?" He spun around in front of me pointing at the trees, flowers and up at the full moon.

"I suspect you will tell me."

He appeared next to me in a blink of an eye and his snout was only inches from my face. He had pinned both my arms behind my back with only one hand.

"Do not push me, my dear." He snipped at me and saliva dripped off his long lagging tongue. "I want to show you something secret of mine."

I had not seen him in such a mood before. He seemed somewhat pensive and reminiscent. I kept quiet and relaxed in his grip. Maybe I could learn more and find out how to escape from him.

He let me go and walked toward a path in the woods. "Follow me, if you please."

I did so, and we walked along a trail. In the distance, I saw fireflies twinkling in the trees and could smell the fresh scents of summer. I guessed that we were back in my homeland, but maybe I just wished for what was not true. I could not be certain.

Up ahead I could see a cabin and lanterns on the porch. Sitting there in a chair was a woman. She wore her hair long, and her white nightgown nearly glowed in the moonlight. My heart beat faster, and I walked quickly along the path. As we came closer to the cabin, she looked up and smiled full, open and true. I ran up to her, incredulous and went to embrace her, but she turned away and I realized that her smile was not for me.

She ran past me and threw herself into the awaiting arms of the Silver Fox.

"Mother?" I did not know what else to say.

She ignored me as the Silver Fox held her in his arms a long moment. When he pulled away, she grabbed his hand and pulled him toward the cabin. He followed her, and I watched them. A couple in love, laughing at the simplest of remarks, and yet serious about the world.

I followed them inside the cabin and I wondered. Where could we be? From how my mother acted, she could not see me, and the Silver Fox had forgotten my existence. His attention never wavered from my mother, and he listened attentively to her stories. Together they sat down on the grass outside, and he held her in his arms. They stared up at the light from the full moon and the brighter stars, and I could see, little by little, the sky start to change color.

"Can you not stay with me?" I almost did not recognize the Silver Fox's voice. He held her in his arms and, with his magic, caused the fireflies to twinkle overhead.

"It is almost morning and I must go back." She tickled him under his chin and I realized that his handsomeness was complete for her. His appearance had been altered and he appeared fully human.

I sat against a tree near them and watched. I had never seen my mother act this way with my father and, the Silver Fox, seemed equally enchanted.

They looked up at the brightening sky, and she kissed him one last time and stood. Her left arm glowed in bluish light. She waved at an imaginary spot in the air and a crack appeared.

"I love you, my dear. Be good until I return!" She blew him a kiss and jumped toward the opening before her.

"Until tomorrow night, my love." The Silver Fox grabbed her hands but she laughed and pulled away through the crack. In an instant, she vanished and the doorway closed.

I came out of the shadows and sat next to the fox. He ignored me, staring up at the brightening sky. We spoke not a word until the sky was filled with the sun's bright, morning light.

"Did you love my mother?" I asked the question without thinking.

He thought a moment and answered with a nod and whispered, "Yes, I did. I do."

He glanced back toward the closed doorway and then jumped up heading away from the house.

"Can you show me more of her?"

He ignored me and kept walking.

"Please."

He stopped and waved, urging me to follow him. I turned back to the cabin and began walking the opposite way toward the house.

"Where are you going?" He had stopped walking and I could hear anger in his tone.

"Stop." He rushed past me and put his arm up. "I command you to stop."

I grabbed his hand and pulled him toward the door. "No, let us go inside."

He allowed himself to be pulled in and everything had changed. A light rain fell outside, and the morning had been replaced by a gloomy afternoon. He pulled out of my grip yet I could see the fear in his eyes.

"When are we?" I tried to look around for some useful bit of knowledge but I only found quiet.

The Silver Fox stood in the center of the room and his demeanor had changed. "Leave me alone." He pushed me away and stood still, seemingly paralyzed.

Around the cabin, I saw tiny mementos of my mother's love for him. Several sketches and oil paintings rested against the wall. The room was disheveled and unkempt. I walked toward the far door and he yelled, "Don't go in there. Don't, please!"

I needed to try. I opened the door and walked through the entryway and the dream world shifted yet again. Attracted and pulled to the room, the Silver Fox followed with his hands crunched up against his mouth and fear in his eyes. The room we entered was pure white. The walls, bed, sheets and my mother rested in bed wearing white. Her face, pale, and the light in her eyes dim. She reached toward him, "Come to me."

He pushed past me and I could see tears in his eyes. Kneeling beside her bed, he took her hand and kissed it. "Don't go."

She began to cry, and the tears streamed down her face. I stood there watching my mother, in a dream within a dream, and she took his hand and kissed it. His face broke, opening in pain, the fox winning, becoming an animal in his grief. His voice was hard and thick from crying. "I will save you. I will draw up the mountains and we will flee in the sunlight. I will. I will. I will it to be so."

From his eyes and hands, the colors of the rainbow poured out in utter contempt for death. Yet I fell back against the wall, from his display of power, and I could see the light in her eyes fading. She pulled at both his hands and placed them on her womb. "Foxglove, I am so sorry." Her voice broke and she sobbed. "I love you."

The Silver Fox felt for life, and he held her hands, tightly. His eyes closed, he mouthed words I could not hear into my mother's ear, being private and true. His wild magic streamed out of him, building, gathering strength and time stopped.

He turned to me, reaching out, "Please! This is why I need you. You can change all this. You can bring your mother back and save your sister. Use your gift to help us!"

He had tricked me and finally I understood his tests. I stood there watching my mother's life fade before me and remembered how she had died in our world. A fever had taken her. I had not known that her spirit had traveled to the Land of the Fey each night to be with her fox and that she was pregnant with his child.

The Silver Fox squeezed my hand and pulled me closer and begged, "Please, help them!"

"But how?" The words fumbled out of my mouth and I watched as my mother's eyes began to close. I would need to decide now.

"There is only one way." He grabbed at me and put his hand on my belly. "Before she fades, you must sacrifice Phoebe's spirit to save your unborn sister. A life for a life! With your magic, you can replace the Fey part of your unborn sister with your daughter's spirit. Then your mother won't die and your sister will also be saved. Phoebe will live on in your sister. Please, trust me, it is the only way!"

The horror of what he asked seeped into me and though I longed to hold my mother again and to see her alive, I could never do so at such a cost. I voiced no words but he saw my face and knew my answer. His desperation rose and he let go of my mother's hand and held me close. "Do this for me!"

He growled and his face changed, teeth sharp and eyes crazed. Understanding dawned on me, as I saw him as my Faerie Godmother, helping me with the Prince, hoping I would discover my witch powers and become pregnant. And then his pushing me toward Henri all became clear. He needed my powers as a Chronicler and that of a child of mine. His twisted plan unfolded and I feared him.

"No, I will not help you!" I pushed him away and ran from the bed where my mother lay dying.

He came after me and let out an anguished cry. His concentration broken, the cabin faded from view and we stood in a field of grass at night with the moon bright overhead.

He held off from coming closer and stood with his hands clenched at his side. "I could not save them. I could not. I could not. I could not." He turned on me and lights twinkled around him in red and blue.

I did not know what to say. "You cannot ask me to give up my child. I will not do it. I will not!"

"But it is the only way! I am Lord of the Fey and I have powers to transcend time and can float through the dew drops on flowers on a summer morning. I can do so much, but not what I want most."

I gathered myself and could see my opening. "My mother loved you. It is not your fault that she died."

He rushed toward me and grabbed my hand roughly. "I can smell her on you. You are her, partly at least, and I wanted so much…" He let me go and shifted back and forth into animal and man, fighting himself, unsure and wild. I stood back, unclear of what to do and how to get home.

The world around us breathed and grew with pure energy and his mood cycled, like the seasons and I pulled away afraid of him. Inside, I sought the core of my strength. The pure, white light of hope and love, waiting for my chance.

The Silver Fox unclenched his hands and reached up toward the sky, calling out in a language I did not understand. He twisted his hands above his head, and the tendrils of War fell down upon the land. He looked out across the world with his bright eyes and smiled. "If you will not help me, then I will bring suffering and death to the world. The tide is coming in and my minions will wash the world with blood."

His crazed smile frightened me. Pulling down hard, I saw the tendrils drip down like honey and he stamped the ground with his left foot, awakening Pestilence from its slumber. He orchestrated the movement of these demigods of despair and I tried to walk away but I could not. Seeing me again, he turned his attention to me and said, "You can stop this. Let us go back and you can help me! Then your mother, sister and I will be together, forever. I will have my family."

"No." My one word response was not what he had expected. I put my arms down at my side and let go.

He roared at me and unleashed his wrath. His face splayed open and pieces of flesh danced and swirled, teeth stuck to tiny sinews of muscle that flew out at me with saliva hitting my face. He unleashed his anger, pure, white-hot and brutal against me. I fell back and stumbled. The world trembled at his anger. The trees pulled back, flowers shriveled up and his eyes looked crazed and encircled with fire.

He waved his left hand at me, and he opened a portal showing me Henri fighting a war in France. Screams of men and splashes of blood filled my vision. With his right, I saw the Prince in a second portal, trudging through mud, seeing the sick and dying all around him. His face determined yet fearful of what had felled his men.

The Silver Fox laughed and the tendrils of War and Pestilence flooded into the portals, coursing like a wild stream toward Henri and the Prince. I watched, unsure how I could help them. Lost in what I could see and taken unaware, the Silver Fox then ran at me and tackled me to the ground, using his claws to tear at my belly. "If you will not help me, then I will take what you love most from you. You will suffer as I have and I ruin all you love."

I screamed and kicked him away, struggling to stand as his claws tore into me. All of my life I had buckled to authority, listened and obeyed, but I knew that today would be different. I faced him and put my left hand out in front of me.

"No!" I shouted the word and put my magic behind the word.

Knocked back by my magic, he rushed me again, and I saw his hands changing. His claws came out with tiny razors in the palms of his hands. Berserk and out of control, there was no humanity in him and I stood still, planting my feet into the earth. All I had trained and prepared for came down to this moment.

I raised my right arm and then allowed both my arms to fall out at my side. I opened myself up and let go. The words are clear and burned into my memory. I spoke the opening words to the incantation that Renée had taught me, "I am of the North. You will never possess me. I defy you, resist you and bind you to this spot."

His force crushed into my power and yet he could not touch me. He was stopped mere feet from me. A look of surprise crossed his face as he struggled to come closer.

From within, I dug deep into my reserve of magic and spoke the second part to the binding spell. "No. You will not possess me. I am of the West. I defy you, resist you and bind you to this spot."

The Silver Fox stopped his attack and chains of light came out of the ground. His left and right legs were pinned to the ground. He morphed, shifted and tried to escape.

My strength was fading but I quickly shouted the third phrase. "No! I say again. You will never possess me. I am of the East. I defy you, will always resist you and I bind you to this spot!"

Out of the ground, a third chain sprung forth and wrapped itself around the Silver Fox. My power began to wane and I reached for my belly as blood seeped from my wounds. I closed my eyes and said a prayer that Renée had taught me. I waited a few moments, holding off the Silver Fox's attack and then saw the sky open up. He tried to speak, but a white light from above quieted him and he stopped struggling. I fell back in awe as descending down, she eclipsed us. She had heard my prayer and had come, settling herself in front of me.

The Silver Fox shifted back, human now. "Justine!"

My mother looked down on him. "No. You will never possess me or my children, children's children or those I have loved."

Tears streamed down his face. "Justine. Please, please."

She held out her hand and finished the last words to the spell. "I am of the South. I defy you, resist you, and with all my love for you I bind you to this spot."

"Please." He reached out to her but a red glowing chain flew out of the ground and trapped him. Four chains, compass drawn, stretched and staked to the ground. "I love you."

My mother walked forward and caressed his cheek. "If you believed, all could be changed. The past can be undone. The present is alive with wonder and the future is filled with such hope. You only need to believe and let go."

"I am sorry for what I have done, but please stay with me. Never leave." He leaned forward, resisting against the chains.

"I never left you. If you had let me go, you would know." She kissed him lightly on his forehead and pulled back.

"Please, don't abandon me." Parts of the fox started to show through. "I was wrong in trying to hurt Sophia. I will take any punishment, but please don't leave me."

"I never have." She withdrew from him. "You lost all hope and used your power for selfish means." He began to speak but she interrupted him. "Remember, all can be made anew. The past can be undone. Love."

"But I do love you. I would give you anything!" He strained to reach her and failed.

"Maybe once you did. Now you only wish to possess." She turned on him and walked toward me.

Though he spoke to her back, he said, "I understand. I will accept my punishment, but I will never stop loving you."

My mother stood beside me on my right. She faced me, and I understood what we had to do. We raised our hands, pointing at the Silver Fox. We had bound him to the Earth. He no longer struggled but remained defiant, refusing to surrender. His eyes never left her. Lowering our hands, the spell complete, he vanished into the ground, trapped until in his soul he chose to be free.

My mother floated at my side, but her spirit shifted, fading quickly from sight. She turned to me and said, "I chose what I thought was right. You are my daughter and I abandoned you and your father. I am sorry for that." She reached out toward me. "Love. If I could ask you to do anything, it would be simply that. Tell Renée that I am sorry and one day I hope to thank her for protecting you."

"I will." I concentrated and with my left hand, touched hers. Our spirits meshed and I opened my heart and let my love flow out for her, for us, for everything. For in the end, when all is dust and we are no more, only love remains. My mother's spirit faded. For a few moments, I stood in the empty field and watched as, without the Silver Fox's magic, the portals closed and the spirits of War and Pestilence faded from sight. The Earth was left fresh and new. A great fatigue washed over me, and I fell to my knees holding my belly. The blood kept seeping from the tears in my skin, and I cried, fearing that I was losing you. A sound on the wind caught my attention and I fell back and listened. Renée's magic searched for me and I allowed my spirit to be called back to her. My head rested on the soft grass and I remember the world shifting yet again.

I blinked and Renée stood before me. I was in the cave once again. Outside the snow still fell. Renée saw my wounds and rushed forward, covering me in warm blankets. Then I faded into a deep, dark sleep and knew no more.

* * *

For how long I slept, I do not know. Renée cleaned and bound my wounds, keeping me warm with blankets and a large fire. She had smeared a thick paste on the cuts and she sang to me as she tended me. I often faded off into sleep and in the morning she sat me up and had me drink some warm broth.

Too sore to move much, I put my hands on my belly and asked, "Is she okay?"

Renée nodded. "She's kicking and is fine. Your wounds are not serious. They will heal in time. You simply need to rest and eat."

I cried in joy and put my hands on my womb. You had been saved.

Allowing me some time to myself, Renée later came to me and handed me a bowl of rabbit stew but I pushed it aside. "I must do something first."

I pulled the covers off of me and saw that I still wore my glass slippers. Renée went to help me but I pushed her away. Bending my leg back, I slipped my finger into the back and the slipper fell off easily. The other came off as well. "Hand me my diary."

Renée went over to the far side of the cave and handed me one of my diaries. I held it in my arms and thought of all I had written. I had come far, but had a long way yet to go on my journey. But today would be a good day. I covered the slippers with a blanket and then smashed my diary on top of them. No longer filled with the Silver Fox's magic they smashed easily. "Please bury them in the earth away from here."

"Of course." Renée took the crumbled up blanket and placed it outside. When she came back inside, I expected her to ask what happened, but she did not.

"My mother wanted me to give you a message."

"I need not hear it now. Rest up." She covered me with the blankets and tended to the fire.

Renée is a wise woman and knew my mother still loved her. I could see the joy in her face. I stared at the fire, listening to the wood crackle and pop and then fell back off into sleep.

January 2

The Silver Fox is gone. I have unshackled myself from my prince, the king and his queen, and I am adrift in a new land. I am a woman and have discovered my power. It is my purest hope and wish that I will be able to raise you and that I will be with you as you grow, learning your words and of your magic. I look back on my journey and how foolish I have been, stumbling along the road not knowing where I should go, what I should do or who I was.

Now begins my new journey. If I could tell you anything, as your mother, I think it would be this: "Find your own way. Do not listen to me."

Maybe I am too sentimental and have time on my hands but there it is. I looked out across the land and I see all that it has to offer and teach me. I am new and awake and alive. Renée and I will stay the winter in this area, using the encampment as our home. When you are born, I will care for you and then, in the Spring, we will leave on a wagon and head west to see all of America and her beauty. The strength of this land will draw me to new heights and of the past, all can be undone. If I but believe and let go, anything is possible. My mother loved me and yet at night she lived with the Silver Fox in the Land of the Fey. She had both worlds and yet reached too high, and in doing so, lost all.

I cannot make more sense out of what she did, but I realize that all is possible. The simplest and most important secret of all I have discovered is simply this: I have traveled long and far, losing my way looking for acceptance in others, whereas I only need to accept and love myself. No one else could rescue me. Only I have such power.

My prince never did save me. Neither did Henri. Nor did anyone else. I feel reborn and new. Alive for the first time with a bright and fresh smile on my face. I will go now. Close this part of my book, not forever, not for good, but for now. The words I need to see are out there in the world. The love I need to grow is out among the connections and people I shall meet. Yet inside, in my heart, I am found. I am no longer Cinderella the maid who cleaned the floors and was whisked to the castle by magic and her prince. No, that chapter of my life is over. I am your mother. I am Sophia. Finally, I am no longer lost but am found.

I will see you soon. I love you. I love you. I love you.

Read an Exciting Excerpt from *Stolen*:

To learn more about Ron Vitale and of the other books he has written, visit his website at www.RonVitale.com.

Learn more about *Stolen*, the next book in the *Cinderella's Secret Diaries* series.

For ten years, Cinderella has raised her daughter on her own in America. But a mysterious witch hunter finds her and gives her a message that the Faerie Queen, Mab, searches to destroy her and he asks her to return to England. Fearing that she will be pulled back into the maelstrom of war sprouting throughout Europe, Cinderella flees and wishes to remain free. Yet with Napoleon now Emperor of France and the pawn of Queen Mab, only England still resists him. Pestilence and war have sprouted throughout Europe and Cinderella's magic powers are needed to defeat Napoleon. The further Cinderella runs from her fate, the more she is drawn back. Her long lost love, Henri, is still ever in her mind and in running she learns of a dark secret that forever changes her and sets her off on a course she might never survive....

Read the beginning of Ron Vitale's *Stolen: Cinderella's Secret Diaries* (Book 2):

I stood on the prairie with land stretching as far as I could see. Such glorious long grass that blew in the wind like a living creature filled with such life. The blue sky and brilliant sun filled me with such great joy. We had found peace and happiness on the road. Renée slept still in the wagon and Bebe played in the tall grass behind me. Though, at 10, she had begun to find my nickname for her childish so I used it less and less often. To my right, the horses are tethered and still resting from the previous day's long journey. The grass swayed and, without warning, she appeared before me having hunted us down, parting the grass and walking out of the air. Fresh from my nightmares she seemed and all of my attempts to shield ourselves from her had failed. I should have known that I could not out run her.

Queen Mab stood across from me, clothed in resplendent clothes, shades of purple and black, holding a rifle pointed up at the blue sky. The grass of the prairie and the leaves from a solitary tree rooted behind her swayed in the wind. She smiled at me and said, "I have come for you."

I had been caught off guard. Bebe heard the faerie Queen and crouched in fear behind me in the grass. "I told you that I will not come with you." Again and again I had fought with her in my dreams, refusing to go along with her.

"Are you so sure?" She did not move or adjust the rifle but her implied threat was clear. "Come with me and let us do this the easy way."

My left hand itched and I had long ago learned to control my powers when in stress or fear. Wild magic would not serve me well against the faerie Queen. "I will not come with—"

Queen Mab lowered the rifle and fired. My hand burned bright and I stood straight and firm shielding myself from harm. My magic would protect me. The sound echoed loud across the prairie and my heart beat fast. No shot pierced me and burned through my skin. I had survived. Raising my hands against her, I concentrated on an expulsion spell. "You have missed. Now leave us."

The Queen laughed and she lowered her rifle. "I never miss." She motioned with her weapon over my shoulder and I did not wish to turn around. Renée stumbled out of the wagon, wakened from the shot, and out of the corner of my eye I saw her running to a point behind me. And then I knew. My hope and brightest star, my poor Phoebe had fallen. The bullet pierced through her neck. I had failed as a mother to protect my own. I ran to her, surging my strength and magic into her, but it would not be enough. Her eyes fluttered and she tried to reach for me but there was too much blood. The blood covered all. I could not erase what I saw.

Standing by my side, Queen Mab waited by me, looking down. She put out her hand and said, "Come with me and I will save her."

I thought of what she asked and took it all in. My Bebe had only moments left to live. She had just reached 10 years of age. I loved her. Renée's calm exposure shattered as she tried to heal my daughter while my hands tried to staunch the open wound in desperation.

Queen Mab offered her hand to me again. "I will ask only one last time." She waited a breath and said again, "Come with me."

And, so I did. My hands covered in my daughter's blood, I stopped and reached for Mab. I did what any mother would do.

Purchase *Stolen* at: http://smarturl.it/ojn0sh

ABOUT THE AUTHOR

Ron Vitale is a fantasy and science fiction author. He has a Master's degree in English Literature from Villanova University where he studied the works of Alice Walker and Margaret Atwood, interpreting their novels with a psychological Jungian approach by showing how the central female protagonists in their novels use storytelling as a means to heal themselves from trauma. He lives in a small town outside of Philadelphia, Pennsylvania.

In the fall of 2008, he published his fantasy novel *Dorothea's Song* as an audiobook on Podiobooks and for sale in the Amazon.com Kindle store, and in 2011 he published *Lost*, the first book in the Cinderella's Secret Diaries series, in 2012 the second book in the series, *Stolen*, was published and in 2014 the third book in the series, *Found* was released.

Ron has since published *Awakenings* and *Betrayals*, books 1 and 2, of *The Witch's Coven* series as well as *Faith*, the first book in the *Jovian Gate Chronicles*. He keeps himself busy by writing his blog, and on learning how to be a good father to his kids all while working on his next book.

Learn more at www.ronvitale.com

Made in the USA
Middletown, DE
07 April 2020